I0538967

DEADLY HOLIDAY

A
GEORGIA RAE WINSTON
MYSTERY

MARISSA SHROCK

CIMELIAPRESS

Deadly Holiday

© 2018 by Marissa Shrock

All rights reserved.

The persons and events portrayed in this work are the creations of the author, and any resemblance to persons living or dead is purely coincidental.

Cover art ©Jennifer Zemanek/Seedlings Design Studio

Scriptures taken from the Holy Bible, New International Version®, NIV®. Copyright © 1973, 1978, 1984, 2011 by Biblica, Inc.™ Used by permission of Zondervan. All rights reserved worldwide. www.zondervan.com The "NIV" and "New International Version" are trademarks registered in the United States Patent and Trademark Office by Biblica, Inc.™

Published by Cimelia Press, Greentown, Indiana

Printed in the United States of America

ISBN-13: 978-0-9969879-3-6

Library of Congress Control Number: 2018906611

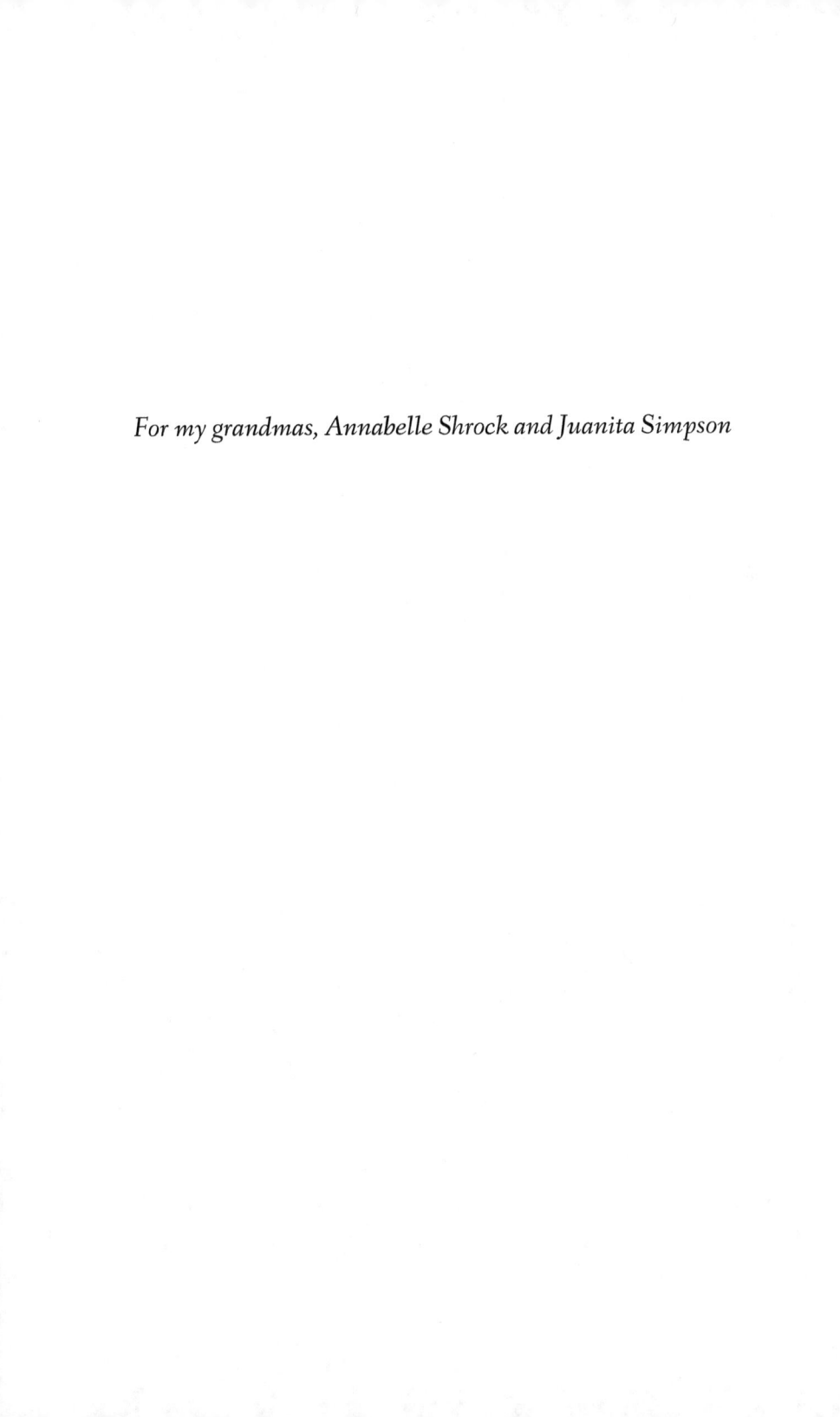

For my grandmas, Annabelle Shrock and Juanita Simpson

AUTHOR'S NOTE

Writing a novel gives an author the opportunity to create new places, and this is something I chose to do in *Deadly Holiday*. Wildcat Springs, Richardville, and Richard County are all figments of my imagination. I also took some liberties with police investigations to remain true to the pace and flow of the story.

CHAPTER ONE

Awkwardness and I were old friends, but it wasn't every day that I found myself wedged under the church secretary's desk clutching my Bible to my chest. Crouching next to a tangle of dusty computer cords and cobwebs, I pressed my finger underneath my tingling nose.

Drop dead, sneeze.

I longed for the superpower of invisibility, because if Pastor Mark and Zach saw me, how would I ever explain? I'd certainly use my gift of babbling to try.

But I should back up and start at the beginning.

It began earlier that night at choir practice, the Monday before Thanksgiving. I was sitting in Wildcat Springs Community Church's chapel and stewing about what to get my boyfriend for our first Christmas together.

Okay, maybe *boyfriend* was a stretch. Cal Perkins and I had been dating for about three weeks and hadn't attempted the let's-be-exclusive conversation. The talk had to be coming soon, right? I wasn't sure, because I'd never had a serious boyfriend—ever. Which, at thirty, was just plain embarrassing to admit.

I drummed my fingers against my music folder.

"Georgia, will you close in prayer?" Jessica Myers, the choir director, faced me with a broad smile.

A few fellow sopranos looked my way, and I squirmed. I swallowed and locked eyes with one of my best friends, Brandi Hartfield, sitting in the alto section. Sure, God and I powwowed on a regular basis, but praying in front of forty-odd people wasn't my thing, and Brandi, a praying expert, knew it. But instead of jumping in to save me, she tossed an encouraging nod in my direction.

Traitor.

"Sure!" I wrung my hands and sent a silent petition Heavenward. *Please don't let me embarrass myself.* "Lord, thank you for this practice and for the work Jessica's doing to make our part of the Christmas program a success. I pray for traveling mercies as we go our separate ways for Thanksgiving and ask that you bring us back safely next week. Amen."

No one sent strange looks my direction, so my prayer apparently passed inspection. Not too long. Not too short.

I slid my folder into my red satchel that I'd bought on sale last week because I'd wanted to be festive for the holiday season. Plus, it looked good with my gray, skirted peacoat.

"Run into any good mysteries lately?" Olivia Scott picked up her folder and tucked it under her arm. She was a pretty girl who was around twenty or so, and we'd had fun chatting during the last few rehearsals.

"No—just the TV variety—thank goodness." I'd recently helped the Richard County Sheriff's Department solve a murder case, and apparently, I was developing a reputation as my home town's amateur sleuth.

"Isn't it exciting to help solve a case?" She brushed a bit of lint off of her black, lacy sleeve.

"Actually—yes." I tied my sash. "But I'm just as happy bingeing on episodes of *Psych*."

Her face lit up. "Totally. I love Shawn and Gus." She picked up her purse. "Happy Thanksgiving." Olivia sailed past me, her strawberry blond hair swishing.

I headed toward the exit, and Brandi joined me. "I didn't blow that prayer, did I?" I whispered.

"You did fine." Brandi flipped her short brown curls out from the black fur collar on her coat.

"Thanks." We took the narrow hallway toward the church's main entrance. "I need to swing by the lost and found because I left my Bible here yesterday." I pointed in the direction of the offices.

Mona Pletcher, the secretary, kept a basket of lost items behind her desk.

Brandi removed gloves from her coat pockets as we crossed the café area. "I'm so ready for a break. One more day."

She taught eighth-grade social studies, and this year's class wasn't exactly stellar—academically or behaviorally.

We stopped next to Mona's curved desk that overlooked the hallway, and I walked around the counter. "I don't know how you do it."

After student teaching, I'd opted out of a career in music education and had chosen to farm corn and soybeans with my grandpa Winston instead.

I spotted my Bible sitting in the basket on top of a pile of sweaters and sweatshirts. As I grabbed it, an angry, but muffled, voice blasted through the office area.

"What were you thinking? What kind of example are you setting for the kids?" Pastor Mark shouted.

Brandi and I exchanged glances, and I started to tiptoe around the desk.

"Just let me explain!" It was a younger man's voice—probably

Zach Mishler. He'd worked at our church for about six months as the youth pastor. Though he was at least twenty-five, he blended in with the kids because of his boyish face. "I have a good reas—"

"Go," Pastor Mark said. "We'll discuss this when I've calmed down."

Pastor Mark's office door flew open. Brandi ducked around the corner, but I dove under Mona's desk, scrunching my long legs into the tiny space.

So, there I was—Georgia versus a mega sneeze.

I pushed harder underneath my nose. *I will win this war.* I peered around the edge of the desk.

Zach stomped down the hall toward the side exit, and Pastor Mark slapped his palm against the wall and muttered something I couldn't understand.

The tingling in my nose diminished, and I dropped my hand.

Shoulders drooping, Pastor Mark smoothed his thinning hair and trudged to his office. When he slammed his door, I unwound my legs, darted around Mona's desk, and half-ran, half-limped toward Brandi, who was already down the hall out of earshot.

"*Achoo!*" My sneeze refused to be denied.

"Bless you. Thank goodness they didn't see you," Brandi whispered when I caught up.

"No kidding." I sniffled. "I barely fit. I've always said I'm too tall for my own good." I chuckled, but then my laughter faded. "What do you think Zach did?"

Brandi flattened her lips. "No idea."

I stifled a sigh. Brandi hated gossip, so if I wanted to speculate, I was talking to the wrong friend. If our other buddy, Ashley Choi, had been here, she wouldn't have hesitated to give me her opinion, and we would've analyzed the situation to death.

Whatever the issue was, I'd hear about it soon enough. Wildcat Springs, Indiana, was a small town, and things never stayed secret for long.

Thanksgiving Day, I stood on the front porch of my mom and stepdad's massive Tudor in Richardville, Indiana's swankiest subdivision, while I balanced a store-bought veggie tray, the safest item for me to contribute to our feast. I rang the bell and waited.

Every gathering with the Winston-Farthing clan had been a trial for me since Mom had married Dan five years ago. And because my brother Dakota and his wife Stella were with her family for Thanksgiving, I'd be very outnumbered today.

Farthings, five. Winstons, one.

My twenty-year-old stepsister Makayla opened the door.

"Hey, Georgia." She flipped her pink-streaked hair over her shoulder and stepped aside so I could enter.

"Nice lip ring." Her new addition looked painful.

"Thanks." She took my coat, hung it in the closet, and lowered her voice. "Dad totally hates it."

No surprise, since her buttoned-up lawyer of a father had been apoplectic about her hair. "Did you tell him it's less permanent than a tattoo?"

"That strategy failed." She rolled her blue-green eyes—her most striking feature.

Makayla still hadn't gotten over the fact that her daddy had brought a stepmom into her confusing teenaged life, and since I understood her conflicted feelings about parents remarrying, we had a comfortable, unspoken truce where we exchanged pleasantries and then left each other alone.

Today was no exception, so I followed the aroma of roasting turkey and sage dressing into the kitchen. For a few seconds, the familiar mingling of smells tricked me into thinking that if I just closed my eyes, Daddy would still be here with us, and my life would be simpler.

Looking at Mom and Dan's remodeled kitchen with its

modern rustic touches, like the barn door on the pantry, I wondered if Mom missed our farm. After Daddy'd died, she'd lived there for a few years before remarrying and selling the one-hundred-year-old house to me.

Mom bustled toward me and gathered me in a hug. "Hi, sweetie." She wore her honey-blond hair—the same shade as mine—short. If only I'd inherited her petite build and love of running. Instead, I carried a bit more weight than I would've liked.

She flitted back to the stove to stir the noodles simmering in chicken broth.

Dan took the veggie tray, cracked it open, and grabbed a baby carrot. "I thought you might bring that detective you've been seeing lately."

My eyes widened. "Cal went to Ohio to be with his family."

Should my relationship with Cal be moving faster? Truthfully, neither one of us had considered spending Thanksgiving together, though we'd video chatted this morning.

Dan ripped the foil covering off the dip and dunked a carrot in ranch dressing. "Maybe we can meet him at Christmas."

"Maybe." Or not. The last thing I wanted was to scare Cal away, but his years in law enforcement had made him tough.

"Meet who?" Austin sauntered to the island, clawed a handful of veggies, and gave me the once-over. Or was it Preston? Dan's twenty-four-year-old identical twin sons both had broad shoulders, blond hipster haircuts, and were—unfortunately—as handsome as they believed.

"Does the old maid Georgia finally have a boyfriend?" He waggled his eyebrows. "Are they going to get married and make little farmer babies?"

Dan was a nice man, but I didn't know what'd happened to his sons. Not only had the apples fallen far from the tree, but they'd rolled downhill and rotted.

"I don't have a crystal ball, Austin, but if I did, it'd show me you'll *never* get married and make babies." I wondered for the thousandth time how he and his brother scraped together enough maturity to make a living selling houses.

"I'm Preston." He winked and shoved a piece of cauliflower in his mouth.

Dan elbowed his son, his handsome face filled with disapproval. "Cut it out, Austin."

Austin snickered and went into the living room to watch football with his diabolical partner in crime, and I made a mental note that he was wearing a black polo.

Ever since I'd known them, they'd thought it was a real kick to try to fool me with the whole who's who nonsense. And I *couldn't* tell them apart. Correctly identifying Austin had been a lucky guess. Probably if I was around them enough, I might figure it out eventually, but I didn't exactly go looking for opportunities to hang out with them.

I lingered next to the kitchen table. "How can I help?" Not that I'd be able to do very much.

"We've got it," Mom said. "Go relax and watch some football."

After dinner, I wanted to curl up in the guest room and take a nap, but Dan would have none of that. Instead, the whole family gathered at the dining room table, dumped out a case of dominoes, and started a game of Mexican Train. Preston pushed the button on the domino hub, and the obnoxious whistle whined through the room, followed by a chugging engine.

"So Georgia, what was it like finding a dead body?" Austin smirked as he arranged his dominoes into a line.

I opened my mouth to shut him down, but Makayla perked up.

"You found a *body*? When?" She huffed and glared at her dad. "I can't believe you didn't tell me."

"I'm sorry." Dan selected a blue train marker and slapped it down on the table. "If you'd call or text more often..."

Mom rested her hand on Dan's arm and shook her head ever so slightly.

Makayla pressed her lips together. "Who was it?" She snatched the glittery pink train marker from the pile.

I traced my finger over a domino's edge. "A girl named Tara Fullerton was killed at the edge of my field, and I found her when Grandpa and I were harvesting beans."

Makayla covered her mouth. "Ew."

"Yeah, it's not like TV. It's completely horrifying—especially when you know the person." I tried to concentrate on lining up a train, but the dots swam together, making it a challenge to match the dominoes. "Can we change the subject?"

"It's cool you helped solve the case." Preston flipped a domino between his fingers. "If you ever need a sidekick, I could be your Watson."

Austin plopped the double nine in the middle of the domino hub. "Dude, I want to be Watson."

"What makes either of you idiots think she'd pick you as a sidekick?" Makayla asked.

Austin clutched his chest. "You wound me, Mak."

Preston pretended to stab and twist a knife into his heart. "No words."

"You can all relax." I caught Makayla's eye and smiled. "I don't need any sidekicks because I'm not planning to find a dead body ever again."

That night, I escaped with plenty of leftovers that Mom had packaged in to-go containers. The drive back to my farm outside of Wildcat Springs usually took about twenty minutes. When I was almost home, my phone rang, and I didn't recognize the number that appeared on my truck's navigation screen.

I tapped the phone button on the steering wheel. "This is Georgia."

"Oh, I'm glad I caught you. Ruby Daniels here." The shrill voice of my church drama director reverberated through the cab.

"What's going on?"

"Have you heard Jessica Myers was in a car accident earlier today?"

I drew a sharp breath and thought of Jessica's family. "No. Is she okay?"

"She'll live, but her leg got mangled pretty badly. Had to have surgery. Poor thing'll have a simply awful time trying to keep track of those kids of hers while she's stuck in bed."

"Was her family hurt?"

"No. She left her little hellions at home and was making a last-minute run to the dollar store when the Saxon boy ran a stop sign and T-boned her over on 850 North and 1000 East. I tell you, that intersection is terrible. I don't know how many accidents it'll take before the county puts in a four-way stop."

"Is the Saxon boy okay?" For the life of me, I couldn't remember his first name, even though his family attended our church.

"His airbag went off, but he walked away with a few scratches since he's got that huge pick-up truck."

I kneaded my steering wheel. "I'll definitely be praying for Jessica."

"Good. She needs it. Anyhoo, the reason I called is that there's simply no way Jessica will recover in time to direct the choir for our Christmas program."

Now I knew what Ruby wanted. *Wait for it...*

"Would you take Jessica's place? I can't bear the thought of letting our community down. They so look forward to the program."

Being the musical director was an entirely different level of responsibility than singing in the choir, and I wasn't sure I had it in me. Still, it'd be good to keep my skills sharp. Agriculture was a tough business, and a bad year could force me to use my college degree. Though, the thought of spending my days trapped in a classroom taming squirrely kids gave me heart palpitations. Besides, with harvest finished, I did have more time to spare.

"I'd be happy to." I forced enthusiasm into my tone.

"Wonderful! Come to the church tomorrow morning at nine sharp. We'll discuss my creative vision, and you can pick up the program binder."

"How about ten?" I wasn't exactly a morning person in the winter when I had fewer farming responsibilities.

"Nine works better for me."

I gritted my teeth. "Sure. I'll see you at nine. Have a good night." I disconnected the call and blew out a breath. What'd I gotten myself into?

The next morning, I arrived at my church and turned onto the west entrance's winding drive. Through the years, we'd grown by drawing people from all over Richard County, and we'd added on to the one-hundred-year-old brick building. There'd been some talk lately of tearing down the old church, but the prospect of seeing a piece of my childhood turned to rubble saddened me.

I made it inside at exactly nine o'clock. Mona Pletcher typed at her computer behind the desk that'd been my hideout on

Monday night. A plate of Christmas tree shaped cookies rested on the counter.

She looked up and smiled. "Good morning, Georgia. How was Thanksgiving?"

I decided to focus on the positive. "My mom knows how to cook a great feast. How was yours?"

"Not bad, even though my kids are with their dad until tomorrow." Her perfectly shaped brows and berry-colored lips reminded everyone she sold cosmetics. She'd taken the extra job when her husband had left her for a newer—though definitely not prettier—model. She motioned over her shoulder. "Ruby's in the greenroom."

"Thanks."

"We appreciate you stepping up." Mona was also singing in the Christmas choir.

"Happy to help." *I think.*

I rounded the corner and waved at Pastor Mark in his office. "Morning!"

"I hear you've been recruited."

"I should apologize in advance."

He scoffed. "Nah. You'll do great." He put on his reading glasses and picked up his Bible.

Zach walked toward his office. Had he and Pastor Mark made up after their fight?

"Hey there," he said.

He probably had no clue what my name was because we didn't run in the same circles, though he'd hung out with my cousin J.T. Simms a few times. He sported a red, long-sleeved T-shirt made to look like an ugly Christmas sweater.

"Nice shirt," I said.

"Thanks. Gotta get in the spirit." He gave me a thumbs up and shoved a Christmas tree cookie into his mouth.

I entered the greenroom, which led to the auditorium stage

and housed Ruby's desk, but she was nowhere to be seen. "Ruby?"

"I'm coming." Holding a pile of biblical costumes that towered against her chest, she lumbered in and dropped them on the couch. "You wouldn't believe how musty these things get in the basement closet." She heaved a sigh. Though her face was splotchy, it didn't hide the fact that she'd used a heavy hand with her bright pink blush.

"How was your Thanksgiving?" I asked.

"My family isn't celebrating until Sunday." She motioned toward her desk. "See that binder? That's the key to the kingdom. It'll be your *life* for the next two weeks." She tucked a strand of her chin-length gray hair behind her ear.

Oh boy. "The program's already cast?" I picked up the binder and flipped through it.

"Yes." She clasped her hands. "I'm taking care of all of the drama."

I didn't doubt that for one minute.

Doug Brockwell, the custodian, walked in from the auditorium. "The lights are good to go, Ruby."

"Yay! You're my hero." She clapped. "Doug and his wife Ella are Mary and Joseph, so their little Lyla can play baby Jesus. It's providential because they sing beautifully."

This time Ruby wasn't exaggerating. Doug had been two years ahead of me at Wildcat Springs High School, and we'd both been in show choir. He had a gorgeous tenor voice.

His face reddened. "Hey, Georgia." He looked at Ruby and shoved his hands into his brown Carhartt overalls. "I'm going to head out and finish setting up the nativity scene." He hitched his thumb toward the door and made his escape.

How long would it be before I could make mine?

Ruby's nasal voice recaptured my attention. "I'm thankful you're handling the music because I couldn't play the piano if someone put a gun to my head, and my voice sounds like a cow giving birth." Ruby's expression dared me to challenge that assertion.

Instead, I blinked. "That sounds painful."

"Ask my husband. When we got married years ago, he begged me not to cause a scene by singing in church, so I made peace with my lack of ability and threw my life into drama."

I half expected her to display jazz hands every time she said the word *drama*. Instead, she opened a closet door, revealing a stackable washer and dryer. "I trust our choir practice schedule works for you?"

My phone buzzed, and I glanced at the picture and text. Mom wanted my opinion on a gift for Makayla. I wasn't sure why she wanted to shop in all of the madness, but she and Aunt Janie loved Black Friday.

Ruby sorted tunics by colors. "I don't permit cell phones in my practices, so I expect that as choir director, you'll set an example?" She flattened her lips and looked back and forth between the offending phone and my face.

"Yes, ma'am." I didn't want to find out what would happen if I didn't, so I shoved my phone in the back pocket of my jeans.

"Now, does our practice schedule suit you?"

"It's fine." I held the binder to my chest as Ruby threw a load of tunics in the washer and launched into an animated thirty-minute dissertation on her vision for *A Time Traveler's Christmas* —the story of a middle school girl searching for the true meaning of Christmas. With the help of her scientist neighbor, the girl traveled back in time to witness the birth of Jesus.

When Ruby finished, I took a deep breath. *Lord, give me strength.* Not wanting Ruby to regret the faith she'd put in me, I said good-bye and hightailed it out of the building before I could be roped into additional responsibilities.

Chilly air seeped under my coat collar, so I tightened my

scarf. Indiana Novembers often produced one overcast day after another, and today was no exception. I didn't mind the short days, because early night hid the dreariness. I needed to get my Christmas tree up soon to add some cheer, and that might be a good plan for later today.

I pulled onto the winding driveway and decided to take the south exit to see Doug's progress on the nativity scene. A truck, with a bed half-full of sheep and shepherd figures, was parked in the grassy area between the stable and the road. As I passed, a flash of bright blue caught my eye.

Instead of Baby Jesus, a body sprawled facedown over the pine-board manger.

My heart plummeted, and I stomped the brakes, threw the truck in park, and jumped out.

Only the noise of passing vehicles on the highway broke the eerie silence. I rushed into the stable and nearly wiped out on the straw spread over the ground. Flailing my arms, I regained my balance.

I shoved the plastic Mary aside. Kneeling next to the manger, I examined the man's flushed face and drew a sharp breath. "Zach?"

"Help," he whispered without opening his eyes. "Burning... so...thirsty..."

"Help!" I surveyed the area in search of Doug, but no one was around. The truck full of figures blocked the view from the road.

Lord, help!

As gently as I could, I supported Zach's head and lowered him into the straw beside the manger. His wiry frame probably weighed a good fifty pounds less than I did. He thrashed his arm and tugged at his bright blue coat as if he were trying to rip it off.

Dodging his arms, I pressed my fingers to his neck and located a racing pulse. With my other hand, I dialed 911.

"Nine-one-one. What's your emergency?" a male voice asked.

"I'm at Wildcat Springs Community Church and found one of the pastors collapsed in the nativity scene by the south entrance. He's semi-conscious, and his pulse is racing. He says he's burning—and thirsty."

"Do you know his age?"

"Mid-twenties."

Zach moaned again, and my eyes fell on a puddle of vomit, dotted with the remains of a cookie, on the opposite side of the manger. A stainless-steel travel mug rested underneath the manger.

"He threw up before I found him—but he was fine half an hour ago."

"Help's on the way," the dispatcher said. "Is anyone there with you?"

"No. There are people in the church, but I don't think anyone heard me yell."

"I'm going to have you place him on his side, so he doesn't choke if he vomits again."

"Okay." I put my phone on speaker and set it on the ground as the dispatcher told me how to position Zach on his side and make sure his airway was clear. "Got it."

"Do you know CPR if necessary?" the dispatcher asked.

"Yes, sir—but it's been a while since my training."

"I'll stay on the line until the ambulance arrives."

"Thank you." *Lord, please help him.* "Hang in there, Zach." I rubbed his arm. "Help's coming."

Zach's eyes fluttered open, revealing dilated pupils. "Anchor," he whispered before his eyes closed.

"You're right—God's your anchor." Tears pricked my eyes.

I feared he wasn't going to make it. I'd never watched the life drain from someone before, and it was a kick in the gut witnessing someone so young with so much potential slip away. "Come on, Zach. The ambulance is coming." I choked back a sob.

Keep it together for Zach, Georgia Rae.

The wail of sirens cut through the biting wind.

Zach opened his eyes and appeared to be looking through me. He lashed his arm around until he made contact with mine and squeezed. "Not. That. Anchor." He drew a ragged breath, released his grip, and closed his eyes.

CHAPTER TWO

I'd adopted my yellow Labrador retriever puppy a few weeks earlier, and Guster—Gus for short—was the joy of my life. As soon as I arrived home from the church, I knelt next to Gus, wrapped my arms around him, and buried my face in his neck.

He wiggled out of my hug and licked my cheek. Then, he raced to the kitchen where he grabbed his favorite rubber ball from his toy basket by the back door, sat, and stared up at me.

I laughed, thankful for the distraction. "I can take a hint."

I opened the door, and he scampered into the backyard, took care of his business, and ran a couple of laps around my lawn mower shed before dropping the ball at my feet. While I launched the ball toward the shed, I replayed the events of the last hour in my head.

The ambulance had arrived shortly after Zach lost consciousness, and I told the paramedics everything I'd observed. The lights and sirens finally alerted Ruby, Mona, and Pastor Mark to the trouble, and they came running out of the building. After the ambulance pulled away with Zach on board, Doug returned from

Richardville, where he'd gone to buy extension cords. With tears in his eyes, he told us Zach had seemed fine when he left.

Pastor Mark assured me he'd take care of notifying Zach's family in Michigan and would handle everything at the hospital until his family could arrive. There'd been nothing left for me to do but go home and pray.

Lord, take care of Zach.

Gus dropped the slobbery ball, and I tossed it again. My phone vibrated in my pocket, and Pastor Mark's name flashed on the screen.

"Hey," I said. "How's Zach?"

Pastor Mark sighed. "I have some bad news."

My heart plummeted to my feet.

"Zach went into cardiac arrest and passed away not long after he arrived at the hospital."

"No." I groaned and squeezed the bridge of my nose. Though I wasn't surprised, given the shape I'd found him in, I'd still prayed the doctors would save him. "Did they figure out what caused this?"

"The ER doctor suspects poison—but he doesn't know how or what kind—especially since Zach has no history of substance abuse. He notified the sheriff's department."

"What?" *Poison? Seriously?* But when I mentally reviewed Zach's symptoms—vomiting, dilated pupils, flushed cheeks, complaints about feeling hot—poison made sense.

He cleared his throat. "Hopefully, we'll know more after the autopsy and toxicology report."

I clenched my phone as my mind replayed details from the morning—and a big one stood out. "The plate of Christmas cookies. In the office. Zach was eating one this morning when I passed him in the hallway, and the remains of it were in his—uh—puke. What if...?" My mind whirred. "Do you know where they came from or if anyone else ate them?" I closed my eyes to squeeze out visions of tainted cookies taking out the entire church staff.

"I'll call Mona right now." Panic edged into his voice, and he disconnected.

My heart raced as I began pacing. *Please, Lord. Protect everyone. No more murders.*

I'd had way too much experience with them.

Gus deposited the ball in the brown grass in front of me, and I stooped to pick it up. This time, I heaved it toward the old red barn.

Nine years ago, Mom had snapped my favorite picture of Daddy and me in front of that barn on his last Father's Day—before someone had murdered him one night at a grain elevator.

Daddy's case remained unsolved to this day, though the sheriff's department and I had attempted to crack it for years. Three years ago, God had prompted me to stop investigating because I'd been ruining my life with my quest for answers. Cal had recently promised to give the case a second look.

After I tossed the ball a few more times, the sky began spitting snow. Gus and I had inhaled enough frigid air, so I coaxed him inside with one of his favorite doggie biscuits. Because I needed to do something with my hands, I started unloading my dishwasher, that I'd finally gotten around to fixing—with my grandpa's help.

My 1980s era kitchen needed a remodel thanks to linoleum flooring and pastel, flower-basket-print wallpaper. In spite of the fact the last update took place prior to my birth, I loved this two-story house with its original woodwork, staircase—and plenty of childhood memories.

As I stacked the glasses in my cabinet, my thoughts drifted to Zach, and his last words haunted me.

Anchor.

What had he been trying to tell me? Had he suspected he'd

been poisoned? Did Zach have an enemy with an anchor tattoo? Was *anchor* a code for something? What if Zach had been hallucinating because of the poison, and it didn't mean anything?

Still, he'd appeared determined to correct my misunderstanding about God being his anchor.

My phone buzzed with a text from Pastor Mark.

Doug, Ruby, and Mona ate cookies and are fine, which is good because they're all gone. Beverly Alspaugh baked them.

Whew. There was no way Beverly would hurt anyone, and it was no wonder they'd already disappeared. I'd known her for years and had eaten plenty of her fantastic cooking. She loved to make meals for our farming crew in the spring and fall when we were busy in the field.

Though I was thankful the cookies were safe, it would've been nice if the source of poison had been that easy to find. I removed my owl coffee mug from my dishwasher and put it in the cabinet.

Hold on.

The travel mug. I'd almost forgotten it'd been lying near the manger, as if Zach had dropped it when he'd vomited. What if someone had poisoned Zach's coffee? I should report it—in case it got overlooked in the chaos.

If Cal weren't out of town, I would've called him. Instead, I tapped the Richard County Sheriff's Department's number. When a receptionist answered, I asked to speak with a detective.

"Detective Kimball is unavailable, so you'll have to leave a message," the receptionist said.

"Thanks." I flipped a strand of hair back and forth while I waited for the voicemail beep. "This is Georgia Winston. I found Zach Mishler this morning. Anyway, when my pastor called to tell me Zach died, he mentioned the ER doctor suspected poison, and I remembered seeing a travel mug under the manger when I found Zach. I thought you'd want to check it for poison."

I disconnected, sighed, and began dropping silverware into the drawer organizer. I'd done my duty.

About an hour later, I'd finished dragging all my boxes of Christmas decorations out of the guest-room closet and down the stairs when my doorbell chimed. Gus beat me to the foyer and emitted a few ferocious barks.

Peeking through the sidelight, I spotted Cal's colleague, Detective Marvin Kimball.

Great. Why'd Cal have to be out of town? From what he'd told me, Marvin was a thorough investigator, but he'd left his sense of humor back at the police academy in 1985.

Grabbing hold of Gus's collar, I opened the door. "Afternoon, Detective Kimball."

"Miss Winston." His face remained expressionless. "I have a few questions about Zach Mishler and the circumstances surrounding his death." His growly voice mingled with the cloud of cigarette smoke clinging to him.

"Come in." Gus was trying to escape my grip so he could give the detective a full-fledged greeting. *Not gonna happen, little buddy.* "Excuse me while I crate my dog. He's friendly to a fault, and I'm sure you don't want him jumping all over those nice black pants of yours."

"Thank you." He stepped inside and stared at me without blinking, and I wished I could rocket back in time and retrieve this dude's sense of humor.

I woman-handled Gus into his crate in the utility room and

tossed in a frayed chew toy. Hopefully, that'd be enough of a distraction.

Brushing the hair off of my sweater and jeans, I returned to the foyer where Detective Kimball was waiting. "Did you get my voicemail?"

"Yes. Thank you."

I nodded. "Zach deserves justice. How can I help?"

"Describe your relationship with Zach Mishler." He unzipped his windbreaker far enough to pull a notebook and pen from his shirt pocket.

Merciful heavens. Had I made myself look like a suspect by reporting the travel mug? I'd fix that—fast. "We met at my church's welcome reception six months ago when he came to work as the youth pastor. I saw him every Sunday, but we never spent time together. I'm not sure he remembered my name. In fact, that thought crossed my mind this morning."

"Tell me what happened earlier today."

"I went to church to meet with Ruby Daniels about the Christmas program. I passed Zach in the hallway and spoke to him. He seemed fine—cheerful actually. He was wearing one of those T-shirts that looks like an ugly Christmas sweater, and I complimented him. When I left around nine-thirty, I drove by to see the nativity scene. That's when I found him sprawled over the manger. I called nine-one-one immediately."

"Anyone else around?"

"No. Doug Brockwell had gone to Richardville to get extension cords." So he'd said. What if he'd poisoned Zach's coffee before he left? Surely not. I shook the thought away.

"Was Zach conscious when you found him?"

"Barely. He told me he was burning up and thirsty. Then he said *anchor.* Like it was important."

"I see." He made another note on the pad.

"I thought he meant God was his anchor, but when I said

that, he corrected me—right before he passed out. Do you think *anchor* could be important?" My last question flew out before I could stop it.

"Could be. It's my job to figure that out."

There was no mistaking the message in his statement. After this conversation, my assistance wouldn't be appreciated. No surprise since I'd been downright annoying in my quest for answers about Daddy's murder. Detective Kimball had been with the sheriff's department for years, though he'd only been detective for the last several and hadn't been on the receiving end of Georgia the Bulldog.

He slid his notebook back in his pocket. "Thanks for your time." He turned toward the door.

I gnawed my lip. Should I tell him about the argument I'd witnessed? Did I want to implicate the man who'd been my pastor for fifteen years? "One more thing," I blurted.

He faced me. "Yes?"

"Monday night, I was getting my Bible from the lost and found after choir practice when I overheard Pastor Mark and Zach arguing about something Zach had done."

He let go of the knob and took out his notebook again. "What was that?"

"I'm not sure. Zach had somehow set a bad example for the kids, and it made Pastor Mark mad. I hate making it sound like I suspect my pastor of wrongdoing, but he might know something, and what if Zach was doing something illegal and someone came after him—?"

"Thank you, Miss Winston. I'll contact you if I have any more questions. Have a nice day." On the way out, he flexed his cheek muscles in a smile-ish gesture that made me miss Cal's pleasant demeanor—and heart-stopping dimple.

Come home soon, Cal.

I'd just freed Gus and set out leftovers when J.T. arrived at my back door, and Gus launched into full-greeting mode by jumping up on my cousin.

"Guster Winston! Down!" I needed to get this critter to obedience school ASAP.

J.T. chuckled as he grabbed the dog's paws and danced with him. "He's fine." He dropped Gus's feet, and his smile faded when he met my eyes. "I heard you found Zach. You okay?"

"Mostly. A little more shaken up now that I've heard he may've been poisoned."

J.T. gaped at me. "That's crazy. Zach and I were going to play video games tonight."

"Wow. I'm sorry."

"Yeah. Me too." He took off his coat and revealed his Wildcat Springs Implement shirt, so he must've come from work, where he sold lawn mowers and farm equipment. He hung his jacket on a chair at my kitchen table. "Good thing we closed at noon today. Not sure I could concentrate."

"Want some Thanksgiving leftovers?" I pointed to the containers sitting next to the microwave. "There's plenty—and I'm not that hungry."

"No thanks. I grabbed a sandwich earlier."

I was a little embarrassed by the relief I felt since the leftovers were about the only decent food I had in the house, and deep down I wasn't thrilled about sharing my mom's stuffing. "I have Coke or water."

"Coke's good."

I took one from the refrigerator and gave it to J.T., and as I dished out mashed potatoes, noodles, turkey, and stuffing, I told him about finding Zach and Detective Kimball's visit, which helped the mental fog of the last few hours work its way out of my brain.

Gus sat next to J.T., and he patted the dog's head. He propped his elbows on the table and rested his head in his hands, causing his man-bun to bob. "Who'd want to poison him?"

"I've been wondering the same thing." Gus apparently decided I needed some attention because he moved over to me. I tossed him a scrap of turkey and filled J.T. in on the argument I'd witnessed on Monday. I put the plate in the microwave and tapped the reheat button.

"You think Pastor Mark could've had something to do with this?"

"No. But he might have insight that would help the investigation if Zach was involved with something shady. Was anything strange going on with Zach?"

"Not that I'm aware of." He rested his arm on the back of the chair next to him. "I didn't know him that well."

"All I know is that he's from the Detroit area, and he's single. What else can you tell me?" I leaned against the counter.

"He was fun. Cool to hang out with." He rubbed his thumb over the can. "Total health nut. Exercised. Ate right." He held up his Coke. "Wouldn't even drink pop—or coffee. He was into herbal teas, which I thought was a little weird for a dude, but whatever." He shrugged.

Coffee lover that I was, I'd assumed that Zach's travel mug had contained my favorite beverage, but it'd probably been tea. "What about his family?" I grabbed another Coke out of the fridge for myself.

"Parents are divorced. His dad and brother own a big real estate agency in Michigan. His mom's a kindergarten teacher."

"Was he close to them?" The microwave dinged, and I removed my food.

"He got along better with his mom. His dad wanted him to

join his company and was ticked when Zach became a youth pastor."

I set my plate on the table and opened my Coke. "Did Zach know how people in our church felt about hiring a single youth pastor?"

"Yep." J.T. scowled and shook his head. "What's a guy supposed to do? Not serve God because he doesn't have a wife? It's not like we suddenly become useful to God once we're married."

"Preach, Cuz." I held up my can, and we toasted. "How'd Zach take that news?"

"In stride. He'd been passed over for a few other jobs because of it, so one day he asked me about it, and I was honest."

"Anything else?"

"His family situation could be why he stuck around here for Thanksgiving. I invited him to Mom and Dad's, but he already had plans to serve dinner at the homeless shelter in Richardville. He spent a lot of time volunteering there."

"Interesting." The people at the homeless shelter might give us a lead because, other than the church staff, they were some of the last people to have seen Zach alive. Detective Kimball would probably start by asking the church staff questions, and if I went there, I'd be in the way. It wouldn't hurt to go and ask the mission employees a few questions about Zach's final hours.

"I know that look." J.T. crossed his arms. "Are you planning to start investigating?"

"Yeah." No sense in denying it. Besides, Zach's family deserved answers, because I knew from experience that living without them wasn't easy. "How about we take a little field trip?"

Solid Rock Mission provided meals for the needy and temporary accommodations for the homeless all over Richard County, but the building was located in downtown Richardville, the county seat. Before we went to the mission, I stopped at a grocery store and loaded up on canned and boxed goods to contribute to the mission—and tossed in a few get-me-by items for myself.

Even though the Lord knew my hidden agenda, I wanted to help because it was the right thing to do. We dropped the food off at the donation garage and asked to speak with the director. The man collecting food waved us inside and told us to wait in the office.

We entered the small room with a paper-cluttered desk. Framed newspaper articles about the mission hung on the scuffed white walls.

A man, who sported a gray goatee and appeared to be about forty-five, emerged from a back hallway. "Afternoon, folks. I'm Jim Phillips." His deep voice would've been perfect for radio.

"Georgia Winston and J.T. Simms." I shook his hand.

"What can I help you with?" Jim rolled up the sleeves of his plaid, button-down shirt.

"We're friends of Zach Mishler," I said. "Did you know him?"

"The youth pastor at WSCC? Sure do. Great guy. Volunteered here yesterday. We fed over six hundred people."

"That's great," I said. "Did Zach volunteer regularly?"

Jim chomped on gum. "Started last month. Sometimes brought kids from his youth group with him. I'd say he's on his way to becoming a regular." Jim studied J.T. and me. "You said *did*. Has something happened to Zach?"

J.T. squeezed his man-bun. "He died this morning."

Jim's jaw froze. "That's awful. How?"

"We believe he may've been poisoned." My words came out with more authority than I felt, and I realized I'd made us sound like a couple of real detectives. *Please don't ask if we're cops.*

Please forget we didn't show you badges. Please keep talking. "We're retracing Zach's final hours, looking for leads. Did anything unusual happen when Zach was serving here yesterday?"

"Like what?" Jim furrowed his brow.

"Disagreements with any other volunteers or patrons?"

"Not that I'm aware of." He rested his elbow on his arm and tapped his chin. "But I wasn't here the whole time because my girlfriend and I were out delivering meals to shut-ins." He walked back to his desk. "Tell you what. My brother was supervising the volunteers all day. He's working in the warehouse. I'll call him in." Jim picked up the phone, asked his brother to come over, and hung up. "Have you tried talking to the young lady who was with Zach?"

J.T. and I exchanged glances.

"We didn't know he brought anyone with him," J.T. said. "Do you know her name?"

"Not off the top of my head, but give me a second." Jim lifted his finger, strode to the desk, shuffled through some papers, and held one up. "Yesterday's volunteer sign-in sheet. I'll know the name when I see it." He ran his finger down the list. "Here it is. Olivia Scott—pretty thing. Strawberry blond hair that reminded me of my daughter Mia's."

Interesting. Were Olivia and Zach a couple? She'd never mentioned dating anyone, but she and I hadn't exactly gotten that far into our choir-practice friendship.

"Come to think of it," Jim said, "the two of them spent a lot of time chatting with another young gal—probably about twenty—who had really long fake eyelashes. Got the impression they all knew each other beforehand."

"Do you know Eyelash Girl's name?" J.T. asked.

"No. But I've seen her around before." He reached for a pen on his desk and wrote on the list. "None of these names I've circled ring a bell. My brother might have an idea." He held it out, and I walked over, looked at it, and didn't recognize any of the six female names Jim had marked. I whipped my phone out of my bag and took a picture.

"What's going on?" A thin man with a long, bushy beard hovered in the doorway and looked back and forth between J.T. and me.

His facial hair reminded me of my theory that there was a direct correlation between the media yapping about toxic masculinity and the rising number of men sporting full beards.

"Zach Mishler died this morning. Might be murder," Jim said.

"Aw, man. I'm sorry to hear that." Bearded Man's voice was as deep as his brother's. "He was a friendly guy. Always had a way of making people feel special." He ran his hand down the length of his beard. "How can I help?"

"This is Tristan." Jim looked back at his brother. "You remember anything strange happening while Zach was here yesterday?"

"No. Can't say that I do." Tristan shoved his hands in his army jacket and looked between J.T. and me. "If I think of something, I'll let you know.

"Thanks." I held out the list of volunteers. "Jim told us Zach was talking to a girl with long eyelashes. Would you recognize her name from this list?"

"Don't need the list." Tristan waved his hand. "Her name's Carsyn Daniels."

Ruby's daughter. I glanced down at the paper. Carsyn hadn't signed in.

"She seems to enjoy volunteering here," Tristan said.

I nodded. "Thanks for your help."

"You're welcome." He ambled out of the office.

I held the list out to Jim.

Jim shook his head. "Keep it for evidence."

"We're not cops," J.T. said.

Jason Todd Simms! Seriously? A few cuss words pinged in my head, and I physically bit my tongue as I handed the list to Jim, who gaped at us like we'd suddenly sprouted extra heads.

"My mistake." Jim put the paper back on the desk. "Anything else?" His tone had grown icy, but I *had* to ask one more question.

"Do any of the volunteers or patrons around here have anchor tattoos?"

"Don't know. Never paid that much attention." Jim narrowed his eyes. "I need to get back to work."

"Thanks for your time." I grabbed J.T.'s hand and dragged him outside to my truck.

CHAPTER THREE

"Sorry," J.T. said when I'd driven a few blocks away from the mission. "The part about us not being cops kind of slipped out. You were killing the whole detective act until I blew it." His ears turned pink. "Am I fired as your sidekick?"

I laughed as I stopped for a red light. "You're way better than Austin and Preston would be."

"Thanks." He grinned. "Though, if Brandi or Ashley were around, you'd replace me for sure. Besides, if Jim were lying, wouldn't he be relieved we weren't cops?"

The light changed, and I eased the truck through the intersection. "Good point. I won't fire you after all." I checked my blind spot and switched lanes. "Did Zach ever mention he was seeing Olivia Scott?"

"Nope. A few weeks ago, Zach told me he was thinking about trying online dating. He was pretty lonely. He probably met Olivia at church and decided to ask her out instead."

"On Thanksgiving?"

"Yeah, that doesn't make sense with someone you just met."

"Unless she had a bad family situation she was trying to stay

31

away from, so she spent her day volunteering instead of enduring painful awkwardness." I chewed my lip. That wasn't a half-bad strategy, but I'd never crush my mom like that.

"Could be."

I tightened my grip on the wheel. "I should talk to Olivia and Carsyn."

"I'd give Olivia some time," J.T. said. "She's probably torn up about Zach."

He had a point, but my gut was telling me Olivia Scott and Carsyn Daniels might be able to give me clues about what'd happened to Zach.

Life Lesson #52: Always follow your gut. I'd picked up my late grandma Winston's habit of assigning words of wisdom random numbers.

We both grew quiet, and though I normally listened to show tunes or choral music, I turned the radio to the local Christian station and sang along with "My Hope is in You."

A few minutes later, J.T. picked up a quarter from the cup holder and flicked it between his fingers. "This is off the subject, but there's something I've been meaning to ask you."

I glanced at him and turned the radio off. "That sounds ominous."

He flipped the quarter over a few more times. "Do you think Ashley would go out with me?"

Didn't see that coming.

Sweet-talking, Kentucky-bred Ashley would go out with almost any eligible, Christian man, but I knew better than to say that out loud—or to speak for my friend. "Why not ask her and find out?"

He shifted. "Has she ever said anything about me?"

How should I answer that? We'd never talked at length about J.T.—at least in that regard—and I didn't want to give him false hope. "She thinks you're nice."

He groaned and threw his head back. "Great."

"That's a good thing." I glanced at him, and his forlorn expression hurt my heart. "I *can* tell you she's not dating anybody —at least that she's told me about, and Ashley's usually pretty open about the men in her life." In the two and a half years I'd known her, we'd shared a lot of laughs—and a few tears—about bad dates.

He shook his head. "Don't tell her I said anything. I don't want it to be awkward at Bible study." He tossed the quarter back into the cup holder.

"I won't." Male-female relationship difficulties were one of the hazards of having a co-ed group, but the thought of being stuck with a bunch of single women without the mediating influence of men was enough to make me want to sit in a corner and suck my thumb.

He gave a half-hearted shrug. "She's too good for me anyway."

"I'm on my way home from Indianapolis, and I'm bringing Indian food for us," Brandi said a couple hours after I'd arrived home from the mission.

Clearly, she hadn't heard about Pastor Zach, or she would've led with that information. I decided to wait to tell her because there'd be time to get into it later.

I hung a Mammoth Cave ornament on the Christmas tree in my living room. "You know me well." Even though I'd grabbed a few items at the store, I didn't feel like cooking—or eating leftovers again.

"I'll be there in about twenty minutes."

"Perfect. Thanks." We disconnected, and I slipped a bicycle

ornament from Mackinac Island on a branch and stood back to admire my handiwork.

For the past ten years or so, I'd been collecting souvenir ornaments from the places I'd traveled. My favorites were a carved moose from Alaska and a miniature pair of wooden shoes from Holland, Michigan. The decorations and multi-colored lights had already added cheer to my house and helped lighten my mood.

Gus watched while gnawing on a squeaky duck, a gift from my mom, who'd gone into grandparent mode the minute she'd met her granddog. He abandoned his toy and sniffed the artificial tree—I liked real ones too much to kill them—and flinched when a few needles touched his nose. Good. Hopefully, that'd keep him from destroying the ornaments.

Still, I'd better not put any of Brandi's homemade cinnamon ornaments within the dog's reach. I finished decorating, stowed the boxes upstairs in the spare-bedroom closet, and went back downstairs to set the kitchen table.

Brandi arrived and plunked the food bag onto the table. Gus stood guard, waiting for us to drop naan crumbs or rice grains.

"How was shopping?" I unwrapped the naan, tore off a piece, and shoved it in my mouth.

"It shouldn't be possible to Christmas shop for twelve hours and not be finished." She opened a container of rice and dumped it on her plate. "I got some good deals on toys for my nieces and nephews though."

"You, Ashley, and I need to go shopping when she gets back." Ashley had gone home to Louisville for the weekend. "I don't know what to buy Cal for Christmas. What do you get a guy you haven't been dating very long?"

"I'm not sure." Brandi dumped a healthy portion of chicken tikka masala over the rice. "Brian and I started dating in the summer and were engaged before Christmas. There weren't many guys in my life before him." She passed the container to me. "Or after," she mumbled.

Her husband Brian had died three years earlier in a car accident. Though it'd taken Ashley and me some time to coax Brandi back into the dating game, I'd recently convinced her to go out with a lawyer and triathlete named Jon Nordmeyer.

I put less food on my plate than I normally would've. "Speaking of men, have you rescheduled your date with Jon?" They were having trouble coordinating their schedules and had been forced to cancel their date a few weeks ago.

"Not yet, but we'll get to it." Brandi dipped a piece of naan in the spicy sauce. "I'll give your gift problem some thought, but if I were you, I'd ask Ashley for advice in that department."

Ashley had more dating savvy than Brandi and I combined. I stabbed a dainty piece of chicken and took a bite. "So, I have some bad news." I filled her in on the day's events.

She rested her fork on the plate. "Why would someone poison Zach?" Tears welled in her green eyes.

"That's what I want to find out." I zig-zagged my fork through the pile of rice on my plate.

Brandi blinked and displayed her best teacher look. "No surprise there."

We ate in silence for a few minutes, but for me, the action was mechanical. Too much had happened for me to enjoy the food, so I shoved my plate away. The leftovers would keep. "J.T. and I did a little poking around this afternoon and found out Zach volunteered at Solid Rock Mission with Olivia Scott yesterday. I've talked to her some at choir practice—small talk mostly. Do you know anything about her background?"

"Yeah. I had her in school probably seven or eight years ago." Brandi tore a piece of naan and wiped her plate clean. "She's a sweet girl. Did her work and stayed out of trouble." She ate one last bite and pushed her plate aside.

"Do you remember anything about her home life or why she wouldn't have been with her family on Thanksgiving?"

Brandi squinted as if she were trying to remember. "Olivia's mom died while she was in high school, and her dad's a fireman in Richardville. She's an only child."

"Maybe her dad had to work Thanksgiving, so Olivia served with Zach at the shelter."

"That'd make sense," Brandi said. "I overheard Olivia say at choir practice they don't have extended family in this area."

"Carsyn Daniels was there too. Do you know her?"

"By sight. She went to school in Richardville. Now that I think about it, I haven't seen her at church for months." She tossed her napkin on her plate. "Are you sure it's a good idea for you to get involved? What would Cal say?"

It was comments like this—and that she was seven years older —that'd caused Ashley and me to nickname Brandi *Mom*. Then, I'd figured out our smart-aleck humor was a painful reminder to her that she wasn't—and wanted to be.

I shifted. "I'm already involved. Zach tried to tell me something, and it might be important." I didn't have an answer for her second question. No—that wasn't true. I knew the answer and didn't want to face it.

Cal wouldn't be happy.

After Brandi left, I cleaned up the kitchen, took out the trash, and sprayed cinnamon air freshener. Christmas musical practice was in order, so I settled at the piano in my living room, warmed up with a few scales, and played through each piece. I familiarized myself with the vocal parts I'd have to teach at Monday night's rehearsal.

Gus lounged next to the bench and lifted his head every so

often as if he were monitoring my progress like a piano teacher. When I flipped to the last page in the folder, it wasn't music.

It contained a list of the phone numbers of all the choir members—including Olivia Scott's.

My fingers hovered over the keys. I interpreted it as a sign that God wanted me to reach out to Olivia. I closed the piano's fallboard, took the binder, and crossed to my phone on the coffee table.

Picking up the phone, I bit my lip. What should I say? What if Olivia hadn't even been notified about Zach?

Surely, she knew. Nothing stayed a secret for long in Wildcat Springs. Just in case, I'd keep the message generic and general.

This is Georgia from choir. I wanted to make sure you're okay. I'd be happy to talk if you need someone to listen.

I tapped send and hoped she'd be willing to talk to me since I'd been the last person to see Zach alive, though I couldn't be sure she would've heard about that. At the very least, she knew I had a habit of poking my nose into murder investigations.

My doorbell dinged, and I jumped like a guilty little kid who'd stolen a cookie before supper. Gus scurried toward the foyer. I closed the music folder and shoved my phone in the back pocket of my jeans. Before I reached the door, I heard someone whistling "I'll Be Home for Christmas."

My heart skipped, and I peeked through the sidelight.

Cal.

I yanked the door open. "You came home early!" I threw my arms around him.

He drew me closer, and my breath caught. As I melted against his muscular chest, I rejoiced again that his height and broad shoulders made me feel petite.

"Got home around one this afternoon."

"Why?" It couldn't have been because of the case. He would've already been on his way home when Zach had been poisoned. I gazed up at him, hoping that I'd been at least part of the reason. "Not that I mind."

He stepped back. "Let's not get into it."

My chest constricted as I shut the door. He'd tell me when he was ready—at least I hoped so. "All right." I managed to keep my voice steady.

His blue eyes searched mine. "You okay? I heard you found Zach." He leaned over, patted Gus's head, and kicked off his boat shoes.

"Sort of." We walked into the living room and sat down on my sectional sofa. "I feel worse for Zach's friends and family than myself." I pulled a throw pillow to my chest.

"Yeah. His mom's taking it hard." Cal sighed and ran his hands through his thick, dark hair.

I swallowed—and pushed aside my own memories of learning about Daddy's murder. "Do you know what poison it was?" Not that I expected him to share many details about the case, but it seemed like a safe topic. Gus plopped onto the floor between us.

"Yes. Thanks to your tip about the travel mug."

I gazed at him. "Well?"

"When I got back, Marvin sent me to the scene, and I found the travel mug. We had it tested, and it contained traces of poison."

"What kind?"

"Now that I can't tell you, but the evidence we've found suggests Zach didn't knowingly ingest it."

I shuddered. "Do you think someone on my church staff poisoned him?" Cal had visited my church but had chosen to attend Liberty Christian Church, a much smaller fellowship in Wildcat Springs.

"Anything's possible."

I stuck out my lower lip. "This is frustrating."

"I'm sorry." He studied me. "I went to Solid Rock Mission this evening, and the director mentioned something about a tall, attractive woman named Georgia and her male assistant coming in and asking questions." He tilted his head and smirked. "Care to explain?"

In my head, I did a happy dance because his dimple had appeared and because J.T. and I might've been on the right track when we'd chosen to retrace Zach's final day. "J.T. told me about Zach volunteering there, so we took donations and asked a few questions. No big deal."

"You were with J.T.?"

"Yes." I laughed. "*That's* what you're worried about?"

"Not worried." He crossed his arms. "Curious. Why'd you feel compelled to investigate?"

I traced my finger along the pillow's edge. "Zach tried so hard to tell me something before he died, so I wanted answers. His family and friends will need closure."

"Marvin and I will figure it out. Don't put yourself in danger."

"Okay." I stifled a sigh. If Olivia responded to my text, I'd handle it as a caring, Christian friend reaching out to help a fellow believer through her grief.

It was such a good excuse, I almost convinced myself it was true.

"Enough about the case," Cal said. "Tell me about Thanksgiving."

I told him about my annoying stepbrothers wanting to be my sidekicks, which made him laugh.

"How was yours?" I asked.

He rubbed the back of his neck, and his expression darkened. "The fact that I came home early should tell you all you need to know."

"I'm sorry." *Should I press for more details?* "What happened?"

He stroked Gus's back with his foot. "I don't want to burden you with my family problems—and I'm not in the mood to dwell on them."

Or you don't trust me enough to confide in me. He might as well have been wearing a *No Trespassing* sandwich board. Shoving the thought aside as the silence grew unbearable, I pointed to my Christmas tree in the corner near the fireplace. "Isn't it pretty? I finished decorating today."

"Yep. I need you to come help me. All I have is a pitiful four-foot tree and a few tarnished ornaments I picked up at a thrift store. Last year, I didn't even bother putting the tree up at all."

"That's really sad." I shook my head. "I'd be happy to help."

"Cool." He scooted closer and put his arm around me.

At least Cal wanted me around, but would he ever trust me enough to share the deeper stuff in his life?

Saturday morning, Olivia still hadn't responded to my text. Had I offended her? That could be the problem. She knew I was after information and didn't want to talk to me. After all, chatting during choir rehearsals didn't exactly make us bosom buddies. We hadn't even reached Facebook-friend stage, and I now completely regretted not friending her because a search of her page—as well as Instagram—had yielded no results thanks to her privacy settings.

Since I was in need of a caffeine infusion, I grabbed my purse and keys and drove to Latte Conspiracies in downtown Wildcat Springs. The owner, Bobbi Sue Miller, knew everyone's business before they knew their own, so she might give me some information about Olivia Scott or Carsyn Daniels. I figured this wouldn't count as investigating since Bobbi Sue would give me an earful whether I wanted it or not.

Town officials had begun hanging evergreen Christmas wreaths from the light poles that lined Main Street. I parallel parked my truck in the first spot I found, a half block away, and hoofed it to the shop, which was connected to Miller's Books—Bobbi Sue's husband's store.

A blast of warm air mingled with the smell of roasting coffee beans hit my face when I entered the shop, and a skinny Christmas tree decked out with alien and UFO ornaments towered in the corner.

Bobbi Sue was wiping down stainless-steel tabletops and waved. "How're things going with that handsome detective?"

"We're going to see Christmas lights this evening." We'd made the plans the night before as Cal had left—without kissing me.

Bobbi Sue had always taken an interest in my love life because she'd never been able to solve the mystery of why I was still single.

"Sounds romantic. He's quite a catch—for a cop." She flipped the cloth up on her shoulder and pushed up the long sleeves of her gray t-shirt emblazoned with the words, *Paranoia Saves Lives.* "I was hoping you'd come in today."

Interesting. "Why's that?"

She waved for me to come closer, so I did. "Did you hear Zach Mishler was *poisoned?*" she whispered.

"I was the one who found him."

Her eyes rounded. "I hadn't heard. You okay?"

"Yeah."

"Are you gonna investigate?"

"Well I—"

"I figured you would. Come on." She motioned for me to follow. "You're getting whatever drink you want on the house.

After all you've been through, it's the least I can do." As she walked around the counter, she pointed up at the menu made of individual clipboards that displayed descriptions of the specialty drinks. Bobbi Sue had woven large-bulb, multi-colored Christmas lights between the clipboards.

"Thanks. That's sweet." I studied the drink options. I loved the Area 51 Latte and the Moon Landing Mocha but was in the mood for something different. "I've been wanting to try the new Elvis Sighting Latte." The drink was flavored with banana and peanut butter syrups.

Bobbi Sue beamed. "The hubs and I had a ball thinking that one up. We've got another new drink in the works, but it's still top secret." She pumped some syrup into a cup adorned with an alien, put it aside, and began steaming milk. "It's so sad how our little town's had another murder. Makes me wonder if law enforcement isn't trying to cover something up."

Bobbi Sue's distrust of cops stemmed from her dad being set up for a crime he didn't commit years earlier. Though he'd been vindicated, her opinion about law enforcement remained steadfast.

I blinked. "Like what?"

Tara Fullerton's murder hadn't involved any shady business with law enforcement.

"I don't know. Just don't trust 'em. I'm keeping my eyes and ears open." She pointed at me. "So should you."

She added espresso to the cup and stirred before pouring in the frothy milk. After she popped the lid on the cup, she met my eyes. "Especially since the Scott girl's up and disappeared."

CHAPTER FOUR

"*Olivia* Scott?" My eyes widened.

"Yep. The pretty redhead. Early twenties. Figure I'd kill for." Bobbi Sue slid a coffee sleeve onto the cup and held out my drink.

I took it. "When?" Had she poisoned Zach and skipped town?

"Not sure." Bobbi Sue leaned forward. "Olivia and her daddy Trent were supposed to have their Turkey Day celebration last evening because he was pulling a shift at the fire department in Richardville on Thanksgiving. Word on the street is she never showed. He got worried and went to her house looking for her. Nothing."

I had to wonder about the credibility of Bobbi Sue's sources. "Who told you?"

"Martha Jackson was in here earlier, and her son's on the fire department with Trent. Ellen Weber told me the same story, and she got it from her daughter who lives next door to Olivia."

"Do you know where she lives?" It might not hurt to drop in on her neighbors.

"Sure do. The hubs and I rented that very same house when we were first married. Two-eighteen Maple Street. Little brick ranch. Cozy."

I tucked the address away as I tried to process Olivia's disappearance. She seemed like a sweet person, so maybe she hadn't poisoned Zach. What if his killer had kidnapped her? Or she'd been killed too—and her body hadn't been found?

Bobbi Sue waved her hand in front of my face. "Earth to Georgia."

"Sorry." I yanked my focus back to my original objective. "One more thing. Do you know Carsyn Daniels?"

Bobbi Sue shook her head. "Can't say that I do. She important?"

"I'm not sure. If you hear anything else, let me know."

"Will do. You're my favorite detective."

I held up the cup. "Thanks for the drink."

I hurried back to my truck and drove a few blocks to Maple Street. A couple of two-story houses on each side of Olivia's bungalow dwarfed her place. The home to the north had a For-Sale sign in the yard. At the house to the south of Olivia's, a man balanced on a ladder while fastening icicle lights to the roofline. A van with *Litchfield Handyman Service* written on the side sat in the driveway.

I parked next to the curb and went to talk to the man, who'd climbed down and was rummaging through a box at the foot of the ladder. "Excuse me, sir? My name's Georgia Winston, and I'm looking for Olivia."

The man, who looked about sixty, adjusted his Colts sock cap. "Well, Georgia, my name's Pete Litchfield, and you're outta luck. She ain't home."

"Do you know when she'll be back?" I shoved my hands in my coat pockets. "She's a friend of mine."

If singing together in the Christmas choir qualifies one as a friend...

"I'll tell you like I told that detective who came around a bit ago asking about her and her boyfriend that got killed. I talked to her Thursday morning. I was outside deep fryin' my turkey when she left around ten thirty or so. She rolled down her window and wished me and my wife a happy Thanksgiving. Didn't say where she was going, and I didn't think much about it. Figured she was off to a family gathering."

"Right. Did you see any lights on in her house on Thursday night?"

"Yep. Our daughter left for home around eleven—we was having a blast playing charades. Olivia's had her Christmas tree up since the day after Halloween, and she always had it glowing as soon as the sun went down. No different on Thursday night."

"And last night?"

"Dunno. Thursday was the last day I seen her."

"Was she planning a trip?"

"Ain't likely. Usually when she goes outta town, she asks my wife and me to keep an eye on her house. She does the same for us—getting our newspaper and all."

"Maybe she asked another neighbor."

"Could've. 'Cept we've always been Olivia's go-to people. Besides, the house to the north is empty—has been for months. Sure wish it'd sell to a family that'll take care of it."

"Pete? Who are you talking to out there? Is Olivia home?" The front door opened, and a pudgy woman, wearing a sweatshirt with a Christmas tree, emerged and looked me up and down. "You're that farmer-detective."

The edge of my mouth twitched. Never heard that one before. "Something like that." I dragged my thoughts back to Zach and Olivia and prayed my laughter, which was threatening to burst out, would stay put.

"Well, I'm glad I caught you, so you can get the real truth from me. That one"—she hitched a thumb toward her husband—"has rose-colored glasses where Olivia's concerned." She tugged on her sweatshirt's waistband as if she were self-conscious about her round tummy.

In spite of my tendency to babble in awkward situations, I'd begun figuring out that this whole detective thing generally worked a lot better when I kept my trap shut and listened. "Really?"

"Oh, yes, *really*." She snarled.

"Now Winnie, I've told you a million times, I think of Olivia like a daughter." Pete dropped a wad of lights back in the box.

"That massage she was giving you last week says otherwise," Winnie spat.

"My neck was stiff." Pete sounded bored, as if this argument were a rehash for my benefit. He looked at me. "She's a massage therapist. Just helping me out and trying to drum up some business."

"Where does she work?" Olivia and I had mostly discussed music, TV, and shopping during practice.

"At that fancy salon and spa over in Richardville. Inspire." Winnie shrugged. "We *both* can't afford to go there."

"Now, Winnie, I told you to schedule a spa day for your birthday." Pete tugged on his sock cap. "Olivia offered to give us a discount on a couple's massage."

Winnie glared at her husband. "Then why'd you go for a one-on-one appointment? Don't think I didn't see that credit card charge from Tuesday. You act like we got money to burn." She wagged her pointer finger at him.

Was there a graceful way to extricate myself from this situation? Probably not. "I need to—"

"Now hold on there," Winnie said. "How's come you don't

know where she works? I thought you was her friend?" Winnie put her hands on her ample hips.

"I've only recently been getting to know her during church Christmas program practices at Wildcat Springs Community."

"Hmph. We're planning to go to that show. Do every year. Guess it's good Olivia was involved, but I ain't sure how Christian she and that young pastor were."

"Why?" I tightened my scarf as a gust of wind blew across the yard.

"Last weekend, he spent the night at her place." Winnie jutted out her chin.

"Interesting." That was very likely what Pastor Mark had been yelling at Zach about. But he'd said there was an explanation and had seemed eager to defend himself. "Did you tell anyone?"

"Sure did—at least as soon as I heard Olivia's boyfriend was the youth pastor. I called Mark Williams and let him know. There's no call for a man of the cloth to be sleeping around. Besides, my granddaughter's in the youth group. I expect the pastor to set a good example."

Pete pressed his lips together, shook his head, and busied himself with the box of Christmas decorations. Was his disgust over Zach's behavior or his wife's?

Even though I'd most likely stumbled upon the reason Pastor Mark and Zach had been arguing, right then and there, I decided to adopt Brandi's gossip policy. I wouldn't believe the worst until I knew differently. Zach's legacy and reputation deserved the benefit of the doubt, so it was time to change the subject. "Pete said he hasn't seen Olivia since Thursday morning. How about you?"

"I stepped out to get the newspaper and saw her car pulling out of her driveway around six-thirty yesterday morning. I didn't have a clue anything was wrong until her daddy came looking for her last night around six after she didn't show up to eat with him."

"Any idea where she was going?"

"No idea. Never seen her out that early before." She tugged on her sweatshirt. "Whatever was going on, it don't look good with her boyfriend dying like that."

No, it definitely didn't.

CHAPTER FIVE

I knocked on the doorframe of Pastor Mark's office. "Do you have a minute?"

After talking to Winnie and Pete, I'd decided it was time to ask Pastor Mark a few questions, so I'd taken a chance and driven out to the church. Other than a couple setting up the café for tomorrow, the building was quiet.

He removed his reading glasses and set them on top of his Bible, which lay open on his desk next to his laptop. An assortment of frames displayed pictures of his wife, kids, and grandkids. "Come in and have a seat. I'm putting the finishing touches on tomorrow's sermon." He folded his freckly hands. "What's on your mind?"

I settled in the chair in front of his desk. "Monday night after choir practice, I was looking for my lost Bible when I overheard you and Zach arguing."

"I see." He blinked, but his pastor-in-listening-mode expression didn't change.

I twisted a strand of hair around my finger. "I wanted you to know that even though I don't think you'd ever kill Zach—or anyone—I had to tell Detective Kimball what I'd heard because I thought whatever Zach had done might've had to do with his murder and—"

"Georgia, I understand. I told the detectives about it myself, so don't feel bad." He leaned back and crossed his arms.

"Okay." I bit my lip as I toyed with whether or not I should share the information Winnie had given me. Might as well go for it. "Did Zach ever explain to you why he'd spent the night at Olivia's? During your argument, I got the impression it wasn't for the, um, usual reason."

Pastor Mark set his jaw. "Georgia, you did some great work on the Fullerton murder case, and I'm sure the sheriff's department is thankful for your assistance. But there are some matters that don't concern you."

"Why? I found Zach, so it does concern me."

"I'm sorry you had to go through that, but some issues should be handled quietly to avoid the spread of gossip."

"And some issues balloon out of control when there's a lack of transparency."

"I won't be discussing this matter any further."

"What if I can help?" I crossed my arms and shoved away the memory of Cal telling me he could handle the investigation.

Pastor Mark sighed. "I've been your pastor for years, so I hope you trust me. It's not necessary for you to involve yourself in this situation—because it's clearly dangerous. I got to know your daddy pretty well before he died, and I'm certain he'd agree that you need to stay out of this." He held my gaze.

I stifled a groan. He'd played the daddy card. That sure was a hard one to beat.

Once I was home from talking to Pastor Mark, I went into my dining room and faced the chalk wall that I'd painted and bordered with reclaimed wood. Ashley, who was a fantastic artist, had sketched Gus in the corner, which still left me plenty of room to work.

I took a piece of yellow chalk from the basket sitting on the sideboard and began by writing *Poison?* and circling it. Then, I created a web with Zach's symptoms. Vomiting. Flushed skin. Thirst. Confusion. Racing heartbeat. Using my laptop, I did a search with those symptoms along with the word poison, but the list of possibilities overwhelmed me.

On to suspects. Even though I didn't want to admit it, the church staff would've had easy access to Zach's travel mug that morning. I wrote Mona Pletcher, Doug Brockwell, Ruby Daniels, and Mark Williams on the board. I added Olivia Scott because it was possible she'd seen Zach that morning before he came to work, since Winnie Litchfield had seen her leave her house around six-thirty.

The fact that she'd disappeared made her seem the guiltiest.

I made a timeline that started with Zach and Olivia's volunteer work with Carsyn Daniels on Thursday. I put the approximate time I'd found Zach on Friday and added the word *anchor*. I wrote Carsyn's name and drew a squiggly line around it because I still wanted to talk to her.

After staring at the board for a few minutes, I decided to get my mind off of Olivia and Zach, so I tackled my outdoor decorations, which included setting up a small herd of five lighted deer in the front yard and stringing lights on the evergreen. I wound lights around my porch's brick support columns and a hung wreath on the door.

By the time I finished, I needed to get ready for my date with Cal. Since we were going to look at Christmas lights at Sycamore

Park in Wildcat Springs before dinner, I chose a warm blue sweater with silver threads, jeans, and boots.

I'd just secured Gus in his crate in the laundry room when the doorbell rang. He let out an angry bark and rattled around.

"It's okay, boy. It's Cal. We like him, remember?"

Gus whimpered as I grabbed my coat and purse, but when I opened the door, my mouth dropped. "Ruby?" Today, she'd backed off on her overzealous blush application, but her eyeshadow was of the raccoon variety.

"Oh, Georgia, I simply had to talk to you. I've been out at my sister's house, and since I was driving by, I didn't figure you'd mind if I stopped." She clasped her gloved hands.

I mind. I mind very much. "What's going on? Is something wrong with the Christmas program?" I stepped aside, let her into the foyer, and closed the door.

I blocked the hall that led to my dining room because there was no way I could let Ruby catch a glimpse of the chalk wall—complete with her and her daughter's names.

"No, no," she said. "I haven't been able to get Zach off my mind. He was such a nice young man. I was starting to think of him like the son I never had and wanted to fix him up with my daughter Carsyn." She withdrew a tissue from her purse and dabbed a tear. "Now that'll never happen." Ruby sniffed. "I was hoping Zach might be a good match since they both liked volunteering at Solid Rock Mission."

I tried to mask my excitement at being handed this opening. "That's understandable. Did Carsyn happen to volunteer on Thanksgiving Day? Because I heard Zach was there too." I gave myself an A+ for how casual my question sounded.

"Oh, yes—since our family Thanksgiving is tomorrow. Carsyn was terribly shaken up when she found out about Zach's death. He might've been her soulmate, and now she'll never find *the one.* I'll never have grandbabies from her." She buried her face in her hands and wailed.

Merciful heavens. I rested my hand on her shoulder. "The Lord must have someone else in mind for Carsyn. She could meet someone at work."

I should've been ashamed of my fishing attempt—but wasn't.

"She's a nail tech at Inspire. Not exactly the best place to meet men." Ruby flattened her lips.

"True." The same place Olivia worked. I sensed a manicure in my near future. I patted Ruby's shoulder. "What'd you want to tell me?"

She raised her head and fastened her gaze on my outfit. "You look nice. I'll bet you have a date."

"Yes, ma'am."

"With the handsome detective I heard you've been seeing?"

"That's right."

"Is he coming here to pick you up?"

"Any minute."

Her eyes brightened. "Then I'll wait and tell both of you my suspicions."

"What suspicions?"

"About who killed Zach. After Detective Kimball talked to me yesterday, I got to thinking, and I came up with a theory. I wanted to run it by you first, so you could tell me if I need to talk to the detectives or if I have an overactive imagination. That Detective Kimball is so serious, he might think I'm a feather-brained old woman. I'd feel much more comfortable talking to Detective Perkins."

"If you have information that's pertinent to the case, Cal will want to hear it." She needed me to tell her that? Why would I even consider taking Pastor Mark's advice and staying out of this case when I kept getting sucked in?

The door opened. "What'll I want to hear?" Cal entered, smiled at me, and my heart fluttered.

Ruby grasped his arm with both hands. "Oh, Detective, I'm thrilled you're here. I was going to tell Georgia something that's been on my mind and ask her if she thought it was important enough to bother you with."

My face heated. I'd solved one case, and now I was an expert? I looked at Cal and shrugged as he shut the door.

"What's on your mind, ma'am?" He took a step back, and Ruby let go of his arm.

"I got to thinking about Zach and who might've had a motive to kill him." She removed her gloves. "A few weeks ago, I was in my office writing a drama for the sermon series at the beginning of next year. You'll have to come see it. It's a modern-day take on the story of Jonah. And—" She twisted her gloves together as a single tear worked its way down her cheek.

Good grief. It's like she's the star of a one-woman show, and her audience has arrived.

"Go on." Cal's voice contained the teeniest hint of impatience.

"Oh, I hate to cast aspersions." She put a hand to her forehead. "Gossip is a sin."

Someone get the smelling salts ready. I fought a burst of laughter. *Nice Georgia.*

"Ma'am, I don't gossip. I investigate," Cal said.

I didn't dare meet his eyes. If I did, and detected even one tiny gleam of amusement, I'd erupt for sure.

"If it helps, I can go in the other room." I took a step back, but Ruby lunged toward me.

"No, no. Stay. I'd feel better knowing you're hearing this."

I put on my coat, praying she'd take the hint to hurry up and spit it out.

Ruby eyed me and lifted her chin. "About a week ago, I was

in my office, and I overheard Pastor Zach talking with Doug Brockwell—the church custodian. He's also playing Joseph in our Christmas show."

"I've met Doug," Cal said.

"Anyway, Zach and Doug were becoming good friends, from what I could tell. They were in the maintenance area, which is next to the greenroom. I *tried* not to listen, but I simply couldn't help it because my desk is next to the vent." She gazed at Cal as if he could absolve her eavesdropping sin.

"What were they talking about?" Cal shifted and took his phone from his pocket.

"Doug told Zach that he was having marriage troubles."

I tried to follow her logic—and failed. "Why would that make Doug want to kill Zach?"

"What if Zach knew Doug was having an affair and threatened to tell his wife?" Ruby whispered.

"You think Doug might've poisoned Zach to silence him." That seemed like a major stretch of the imagination. If that were the case, then how did Olivia's disappearance figure in? Unless Zach had told her Doug's secret, and Doug had killed her too.

"Exactly." Ruby pursed her lips. "I don't want to think that of Doug, but what if he's hiding something? He's been awfully quiet lately—though he's never been a talker."

That last part was true. During show choir rehearsals in high school, I'd been the one to jabber while we'd practiced our dance moves.

Cal nodded as he typed. Had he temporarily taken up acting? "Did you hear anything else?" he asked.

"No. My phone rang right when Doug started discussing the juicy details." She heaved a sigh worthy of a cheesy TV movie. For all her pretense about not casting aspersions, she sure was enjoying this. She looked back and forth between Cal and me.

"Ma'am, I assure you we're doing everything we can to find

Zach's murderer." Cal rested a hand on her shoulder as he locked his phone screen and put it in his pocket. "Thanks for the information." His smile didn't reach his eyes.

"My pleasure. I'm glad to be rid of that terrible burden. I'm ashamed for not thinking of it when Detective Kimball talked to me, but I was flustered." Ruby slipped on her gloves. "I'll be on my way, so you can get to your date. I'll see you at church tomorrow, Georgia." She sailed out the door as if the admission truly had lightened her load.

I closed the door and leaned against it. "I don't know what to say." I shook my head. "This isn't how I envisioned our date starting."

"It's not your fault."

"What do you think of Ruby's information?"

He shrugged. "Marvin talked to everyone on staff at your church yesterday—including Doug. She's right about the fact that Doug and Zach were friends."

"What if she's trying to keep suspicion off of herself?"

"The thought crossed my mind, but my gut says Ruby is most likely just a busybody since the evidence is pointing elsewhere."

Good to know. "What about Doug?"

"No comment."

Interesting. "Were you actually taking notes?"

"I plead the fifth." He winked.

I laughed as I buttoned my coat. "One more thing, and then I promise I won't say anything more about the case. Tonight, at least."

He quirked an eyebrow. "Yes, Detective Winston?"

"Have you located Olivia Scott?"

Cal's face grew serious. "No, but she's a person of interest, so we'd like to talk to her as soon as possible."

"Because she might've killed Zach?"

"I can't tell you anything else." His eyes gleamed.

"Rats." No surprise there.

Cal grinned. "Ready for Christmas lights?"

Every Christmas Wildcat Springs officials set up a huge light display that began in Sycamore Park and continued down the Wildcat Trail. Since the paved path wound around the Sycamore Hills subdivision before it led out of town, many of the home-owners put up light displays in their backyards for people to enjoy. Besides spending some quality time with my favorite detective, I had another major goal for the evening—Operation Find-Out-What-Cal-Wants-for-Christmas.

At the trailhead, Santa and Mrs. Claus wished us a Merry Christmas and handed us each a candy cane, which we unwrapped as we walked. A partridge perched in a pear tree started the "Twelve Days of Christmas" light exhibit. Two rowdy boys—who were probably about six and eight—ran and skipped down the trail ahead of their parents who strolled hand-in-hand a few yards behind.

"I used to get that excited for Christmas." Cal chuckled.

"What was the best Christmas present you got when you were a kid?" I stuck the candy cane in my mouth and savored the peppermint.

We passed four lighted calling birds before he answered. "When I was in fifth grade, I was into LEGO bricks. My parents got me the police headquarters set." He took my hand. "They also bought the police boat and helicopter, so I was pretty stoked about having law enforcement in the town I'd built. What about you?"

"My piano. It wasn't a typical gift for a kid, but Mom and Daddy bought it when I was nine, because I'd been taking lessons for about six months and had been practicing at my grandma and grandpa's house. Once my parents figured out I was serious, they invested."

"Cool. When will I get to hear you play?"

"I'm sure we can arrange a private concert soon." I met his intense gaze. *Will he finally kiss me tonight?* I glanced at the eleven pipers piping.

"I'll look forward to that." He squeezed my hand.

On our right, twelve drummers pounded away on their glowing drums. "What's on your Christmas list this year?" I asked. Nothing like getting in there and asking.

He took a bite of candy cane and crunched for a few seconds. "Haven't thought about it. I don't need anything."

Who didn't need *anything?* And could he seriously not take a hint? We passed a family of inflatable snowmen. I couldn't give up yet. "Doesn't your family want to know what to get you?"

He shrugged. "Not really. Mom and Dad always give me money. My sister Danielle and I don't give each other gifts because it got so we were trading money."

"In other words, you don't have to do any Christmas shopping."

"Pretty much. I get Mom and Dad something, but that's it. I give my sister money to buy stuff for her kids. Makes my life easier."

No wonder he wasn't taking the hint. Would he even think to get me a present? Maybe I shouldn't bother getting him anything at all. That didn't feel right though.

We passed an elderly couple who were holding hands. If Cal and I got married, would he still hold my hand after we'd been married for years? But I was getting way ahead of myself. I shoved the thought away and focused on the gift-giving crisis.

"Do you have a lot of shopping to finish?" he asked.

"About half. There are several people in my life who are hard to buy for." *Hint, hint.*

"Like your stepbrothers?"

"Yep." I wrestled back a giggle at his helpful—but clueless—expression. "They're not very good at giving me ideas." On our right, an elf dashed toward Santa's workshop.

"That's frustrating. You could quit exchanging gifts—or have a ten-dollar white elephant like my dad's family does."

"I wouldn't want to be stuck with whatever gifts Preston and Austin might come up with."

"Good point. No gifts would probably be best."

Apparently. I surrender—for now.

CHAPTER SIX

S unday afternoon the Winston clan got together for our Thanksgiving and Christmas celebration at Grandpa's house, and his girlfriend Wanda did the cooking. Once again, I'd been relegated to veggie tray duty. Someday I'd learn how to cook well enough to graduate to green bean casserole.

While playing board games, my cousins and I had spent a good deal of time speculating how long it'd be before Grandpa popped the question to Wanda.

My guess was Christmas.

I always enjoyed this family get together, so it was late when I made it home, and I didn't have any time to think about the case.

Monday, I wanted to squeeze in a manicure with Carsyn Daniels at Inspire. Instead, I was a responsible adult and spent the day with our farmhand Cory, hauling loads of corn to the elevator to sell. Late that afternoon, I rushed home to review the Christmas program music, so I wouldn't look like a novice while leading rehearsal that night.

I arrived at church by 6:30 and went to the chapel where we

held our practices. There were still two numbers Jessica hadn't practiced with us, and we'd have to tackle those tonight.

I was laying out the sheet music when I overheard two ladies talking in the hall outside. One of them said something about murder, so I crept over and peered around the corner into the hallway.

"I heard Zach Mishler was getting chummy with that Scott girl." A woman with a double chin clutched a teal-colored Coach purse. "Not sure how smart it was for a pastor to be dating a church member."

The skinny lady wearing hoop earrings put her hand up beside her mouth. "*I heard Mona Pletcher liked to flirt with him.*"

"I suppose if you look like Mona, you can get a younger man. I wouldn't know what that's like." Double Chin pursed her lips.

Meow. I bet you don't. I rolled my eyes, walked back to the music stand, and opened my folder. Nothing like letting the claws come out at church. Now that I was director, I should probably learn their names, but at that moment, I didn't care.

I looked up from my sheet music and made eye contact with Mona who stood frozen in the doorway that connected to the backstage area. Her fourteen-year-old daughter Leah, the young lead in the musical, was bowing her head over her phone. Evidently, they'd taken a shortcut from the offices through the auditorium, and judging from Mona's pained expression, she'd overheard the gossipers. I hoped Leah hadn't.

"Good evening, ladies." I pointed to the pages of music I'd stacked in piles on the front row of chairs. "Come get one of each."

Mona turned to her daughter. "I meant to get a throat lozenge out of my desk. Will you go grab one? Top right drawer."

Leah glanced up from her screen. "Sure." With her ponytail flipping, she bounded out of the room.

Mona moved down the row and picked up the pages. "Did you hear those women?"

"Yeah. I'm sorry."

She stopped and drew the stack of music to her chest. "Zach was a kind man who was wise beyond his years."

I tamped down the surge of excitement I felt at the fact that she was opening up. No need to spook her by appearing too eager. "How so?" Would Pastor Mark have used the word *wise* to describe Zach?

Mona sat in one the rows I'd designated for the sopranos, snapped open the three-ring binder, and began adding the music. "My divorce was brutal on my kids." Tears sparkled in her eyes. "I never wanted my marriage to end. I fought as long as I could, but my ex-husband was determined to be with his mistress. They got married a few months ago."

"I'm so sorry." The words seemed inadequate, but I didn't know what else to say.

"I never felt like you judged me." She tucked a stray hair behind her ear. "Unlike a lot of women in this church." She did nothing to disguise the bitterness in her tone. "Anyway. Zach advised me about how to help my kids—since he'd been through his parents' divorce. That's all. There was never anything romantic between us. We always had a brother-sister vibe going on. Besides, I've been seeing someone else, but we've been keeping it quiet."

It took everything I had to bite back the urge to ask who she was dating. "You don't have to explain yourself to me." *But I'm not sad that you are.*

"I want someone else to know my side. Who knows what kind of rumors are floating around?" She flicked her gaze toward the hall where Double Chin and Skinny had yet to emerge.

As I moved from behind my music stand, I decided to shift

directions. "You saw Zach almost every day. Did he seem upset about anything lately?" I sat beside Mona.

She ran her finger along the folder's edge. "Mark and Zach weren't getting along—and hadn't been for a while."

"Why?" There had to be more than the recent argument.

Mona bit her lip and glanced over her shoulder. "If I tell you something, do you promise not to repeat it?" she whispered.

"If it's about the case, I might have to say something to Detective Perkins," I whispered.

"Fine—but no one else." She closed her folder and rested her hands on it. "Six months ago, when the search committee was looking to fill the youth pastor's position, I had to record the meeting minutes." Mona shook her head. "Mark wanted to hire his son-in-law, Dax, instead of Zach and tried to influence the search committee by bringing up concerns about Zach not being married. It didn't work because the committee members were afraid Dax would spend too much time focusing on taking over for Mark when he retired—instead of concentrating on youth ministry. Mark also said he sensed Zach wasn't passionate enough about youth ministry."

I toyed with this new information while refusing to think the worst about my pastor. His son-in-law not getting a job in our church hardly seemed motive for murder. I'd ponder that later. Right now, I needed to keep Mona talking. "Did Zach ever find out?"

"*I* never told him, and I hope our committee members would have more discretion than to repeat that information."

Either they hadn't been discreet, or the unmarried youth pastor thing had been a universal concern. "Do you know who Zach was dating?"

"He'd been out a few times with Olivia Scott, but I don't know if it was serious. Ruby was determined to set him up with her daughter, Carsyn." Mona grimaced. "That would've been a horrible match."

"Why?"

"I'll stick with facts, because I don't want to be like those two old biddies in the hallway." She leaned aside and glanced over my shoulder. "Carsyn's been exploring different religions to find the right truth for herself."

"Gotcha." That relationship wouldn't work for a pastor who preached absolute truth—or at least I thought that's what Zach had stood for.

Mona shifted. "Zach was still trying to figure out where he fit. He appreciated J.T. hanging out with him."

Choir members were beginning to filter in. "One more question," I said.

"Yeah?"

"Did Zach ever mention *anchor*?"

Mona furrowed her brow. "No. That doesn't ring a bell." A group of women walked closer to us. "Please don't tell anyone about our conversation," she whispered.

I winked. "What conversation?"

When I woke up Tuesday morning, the first thought that charged into my decaffeinated brain was that Cal had never called. On Sunday when we'd talked, he'd promised he'd call on Monday night, and I'd fallen asleep watching *Diagnosis Murder* reruns and waiting.

Patting my nightstand until I gripped my phone, I prayed for a message.

Sorry. Got tied up at work. I'll call another time.

That was vague. Was he trying to send a signal that he was no longer interested? Was that why he wouldn't tell me about Thanksgiving and hadn't taken the hint about a Christmas gift?

I wouldn't think the worst until I knew for sure. He was probably just busy with Zach's case.

Heaving a sigh, I burrowed under the covers. Now what?

Kelsey.

I sat up and tossed my comforter aside. Why hadn't I thought of getting her advice sooner?

In spite of a rocky start to our friendship, Cal's cousin Kelsey and I had become prayer partners prior to her leaving to work at a clinic in Ethiopia. Maybe she could give me some insight if I emailed her. Before she'd left, she made it clear she wanted to hear from her friends on a regular basis to combat homesickness.

A prick of guilt needled me when I realized I'd only contacted her once. Leave it to me to remember to follow through as soon as I needed something.

Pushing the thought away, I got out of bed, put on my slippers, and shuffled to my office. I emailed Kelsey an update about my life, asked several questions, and ended with a plea for help understanding Cal and for suggestions on what to get him for Christmas.

With that mission accomplished, I made a nail appointment with Carsyn Daniels at Inspire Salon & Spa in Richardville and hit the shower.

"I'm glad you came in," Carsyn said a couple of hours later as she led me to her station. The place had a modern vibe with gray-toned wood floors and acrylic and chrome styling chairs. The minimalist style contrasted with the homey feel of Sassy Salon in

Wildcat Springs, where I had my long hair trimmed on a semi-regular basis.

Carsyn had used a much lighter touch on her makeup than her mom, but I understood why Jim Phillips had noticed her eyelashes, which had to be extensions.

She examined the bottle of deep red polish I'd chosen. "This will be pretty. Traditional, but pretty." She set it on the glass-topped manicure table and motioned for me to have a seat.

"I thought so." I sat and held out my hands. Working with farm equipment meant fancy nails weren't a priority, so I'd probably had a total of three manicures in my entire life. Neat, clean, and short had always been my preference.

Besides, there was nothing more annoying than fingernails clicking against piano keys. When I was growing up, my teacher had kept nail clippers handy for anyone who violated her no clicking rule, and fear of having to use community trimmers had ingrained in me the habit of weekly filing.

Carsyn picked up my hand and used a file to shape my nails. "How's the musical going?" Her eyes gleamed, as if she understood it wasn't easy.

"Great. I'm excited to see everything come together." This was true, but I forced some enthusiasm into my tone, because it wasn't like I was going to talk smack about Ruby to her daughter.

"Mom totally guilted me into helping her." Carsyn rolled her eyes. "Told me that if I could volunteer at Solid Rock Mission, I could surely help family with a church program." She set aside the file and put my hands in a finger bowl. "Even though church isn't my thing anymore."

I considered what Mona had told me. "Why not?"

Carsyn sighed. "It doesn't work for me. I can't believe in a God who sends people to hell." She grimaced. "There's got to be a better way." Her posture tensed, and her expression dared me to argue with her.

I shifted. What could I say that she hadn't already heard from her mom? Still, I worried about her eternal fate. *Lord, what should I do?*

Pray for her.

I took a deep breath and remembered my study of Ecclesiastes during small group. *A time to be silent and a time to speak.*

Apparently, God wanted me to keep my mouth shut and change the subject. "Tell me about your volunteer work."

Carsyn relaxed her shoulders. "It's no biggie. Just helping out serving meals. It makes me feel good to give back to the community. If you're interested, you could pitch in. We always need more volunteers."

"I'll keep that in mind." I twisted my foot around the chair leg. "I hate to be too nosy, but has anyone around here heard from Olivia Scott?"

"No." She lowered her voice. "Believe me, all of us are totally freaking—especially since Zach was murdered, and they'd been hanging out."

"Was anything bothering her before she disappeared?"

"No. I'd never seen her happier." Carsyn lifted my hands out of the bowl and set it aside. "She was super excited about Zach. He was a nice guy. I got to know him at Solid Rock. Mom bugged me non-stop about dating him, even though I kept telling her it was never going to happen." She began pushing back my cuticles. "I'm sure you can't possibly picture her nagging me."

I chuckled and bit my tongue—in case a snarky comment developed a mind of its own and charged forth. *A rare win for Nice Georgia.* "How long had Zach and Olivia been seeing each other?"

"I think a few weeks." Carsyn shrugged. "But they could've been dating longer and keeping it on the down low, which I'd understand. Olivia was pretty open about stuff, but Zach didn't talk about his personal life."

Interesting that Carsyn had said that Olivia *was pretty open* instead of *is pretty open*. She kept working on my nails, seemingly unaware of her verb tense choice.

"How'd Zach seem before he died?"

"Happy. Like Olivia." She stopped. "Hold on. There's one thing. I'd better call that hot detective who came in here asking about Olivia."

Hot detective. I curled up my toes and fought a wave of jealously. She resumed cuticle work and seconds ticked by. *Seriously? Don't leave me hanging.* Should I ask and risk looking overly eager?

"Thanksgiving Day, when we were at the mission, Zach got a call while we were cleaning up after dinner." She set her cuticle pusher aside. "He walked over into the corner of the dining room to talk, which I didn't think anything about until his face got red, and he started clenching his fist."

"Could you hear anything?"

"He said something like, 'He didn't waste any time, did he?'"

"Any idea what he was talking about?"

"No." She shook her head. "He must've realized how loud he'd been because he started talking more quietly." She squeezed some lotion on my right hand and started a massage. "That's all I remember. Other than that, the dinner was awesome, and the people were totally stoked about the food."

"How many people witnessed the call?"

"Me and probably four other volunteers? Almost everyone had left."

"Where was Olivia during all of this?"

"The restroom." Carsyn picked up my left hand and massaged it.

"Did you ask Zach about it?"

"Nope. Meddling is my mom's thing—not mine." A bitter

chuckle escaped her lips. "He came over and finished helping me wipe off tables—like nothing had happened."

No matter what, Carsyn's information seemed important. "You should definitely contact Detective *Kimball*."

———

After Carsyn finished my manicure, I invited Ashley to lunch in Richardville since I needed advice about Cal and wanted to get my mind off the case. I chose Kyoto Cuisine, because we both enjoyed the place and Brandi hated it, so it wasn't an option whenever she ate with us. When I arrived, I secured a booth in the back corner near the sushi bar.

A few minutes later, Ashley blew in. "It's been a while since I got a lunch nine-one-one." She plopped her purple and gold handbag—a birthday gift from her grandma in Korea—on the bench. "Are you okay?"

"Mostly."

"Hold. The phone." Ashley grabbed my hand and examined my nails. "Did you get a *manicure*?" Ashley's jaw dropped.

"Yes." My face burned as I pulled my hand away. Apparently, I needed to visit a salon more often.

"Very interesting—and pretty." She narrowed her eyes. "Cal?"

"It never hurts to look your best." I unfolded my napkin and spread it in my lap. "How was Thanksgiving?"

"Fine." She picked up a menu and studied it.

I waited for her to say more, but she continued to focus on the menu like she'd have to pass a test over its contents. Weird. Ashley usually had more to say.

Life Lesson #29: Always take a hint.

I read the menu. Should I get a chicken or beef bento box?

The salmon box was out. That repulsive, pink meat was on the short list of foods I never touched.

Ever.

"Well? Are you going to tell me what's going on?" She slapped the menu shut.

"I don't know what to get Cal for Christmas." When I said the words aloud, I cringed because of how pathetic they sounded, but it was easier than admitting that I wasn't sure if the guy I was dating was into me.

Ashley didn't flinch, which made me wonder if she was accustomed to my shallowness. "Have you asked him what he wants?"

"Yes." I relayed the unhelpful conversation Cal and I'd had in the park.

She drummed her lavender-colored nails against the table. "How about getting him a LEGO set to remind him of his childhood?"

"Are you kidding me? He's a grown man."

She folded her hands. "Hon, a lot of grownups love LEGOs."

"I don't think Cal's one of them."

"Okay. How about concert tickets?" She flipped her black hair over her shoulder.

"Cal doesn't seem like a concert-y type of guy."

The waiter came over, set cups of miso soup in front of us, and we ordered bento boxes—chicken for me and beef for Ashley. She knew better than to eat salmon in front of me. She tried once, and I hadn't been able to stop gagging.

Ashley swallowed a spoonful of soup. "You could get a gift certificate for a few rounds of golf."

"Neither one of us see the point of chasing a tiny ball around a pasture." That's what my grandpa had always said when Daddy had taken time to play.

70

"You don't know what you're missing." Ashley pursed her lips. "Does he like to read?"

"I'm not sure." I picked up my spoon.

Her eyes widened. "Shut the front door. You've never talked about books?"

"No. I don't exactly read much—except for *People* magazine every week." Reading was probably something I should do better about, but I couldn't help it. I preferred movies and TV—especially shows with detectives.

"Georgia Rae, how are we even friends? You think golf is stupid, and you hate reading."

"I don't *hate* reading. I'm just not into books."

"I have a whole library in my spare room if you decide to start."

I stirred the soup. "Thanks."

"What about using his apartment for clues?"

I hesitated but decided to go with the truth. "He's never invited me over."

"Really?"

I ignored the cynical edge in her tone. "I've got to get the gift right. He's the first guy I've ever been serious about."

"What about Evan?"

He was another member of our Bible study group and a high school guidance counselor I'd had a crush on for several years before I met Cal. "We were never meant to be more than friends."

"Are you sure?"

"Yes. Why are you asking me that now?"

"You shouldn't have to try so hard in your relationship with Cal."

"I'm not trying too hard." I glared at her.

"Whatever." She held up her hands in surrender. "I've just

been wondering if you wrote Evan off too soon, especially now that Kelsey is in Ethiopia. Who knows if she'll even come back? I don't think Evan intends to join her."

I'd never seen Ashley use truth—or what she believed to be truth—like a hammer before.

I met her eyes. "I'm sure about Evan, and I'm pretty certain he feels the same since we talked about it." Something else was going on with her. "Are things okay at work?"

She shrugged. "Just fine. Same old same old." Ashley was an engineer at a company in Richardville.

"Did something happen when you went home?"

"Wildcat Springs is my home." She folded her hands on the table and drilled me with a stare.

Okay then. Bad family Thanksgivings must be contagious. Clearly, the subject was closed, and I needed to move on. However, she was in no mood for me to hint around about J.T., and I wasn't about to ruin his chances because of lousy timing.

"I've been looking into Zach's murder."

"Brandi told me you found him." She leaned back. "What've you learned so far?" She scooted forward and widened her dark eyes. "Wait. Is *that* why you got a manicure? Because of the case?"

"Detective Choi for the win." I applauded quietly and gave her a quick summary of finding Zach and everything I'd figured out. "It freaks me out that Olivia is missing. Not to mention that Ruby thinks Doug might've done it to keep Zach quiet about an affair, and I have to admit, it doesn't look good that Pastor Mark and Zach weren't getting along."

"No kidding. What about Zach's last words?"

"No one seems to have any idea what Zach meant when he said *anchor*, but maybe he was hallucinating."

"Wait a sec." Ashley tilted her head. "I've heard *anchor* used in a business name." She squinted and concentrated for a few seconds before snapping her fingers and pointing at me. "There's an Anchor Recovery Center here in Richardville. I overheard one of my coworkers mention it last week."

"Recovery from what?"

She held up her index finger, spoke the name into her phone, and studied the results. "Got it." She showed me. "Anchor Recovery Center specializes in helping people overcome gambling addiction by using a combination of group and individual therapy."

My brain began churning with ideas as I dug my phone from my purse. "What if Zach had a gambling addiction, or he was helping Olivia because *she* had a problem? Maybe that's why she disappeared." I did my own search and studied the website.

"To escape a bookie?" Ashley took a drink of water. "Could be."

I picked *Group Sessions* from the menu options. "Did you see the schedule for the group therapy sessions? There's a meeting at seven tonight."

For the second time, Ashley's jaw dropped. "Hon, you're not *seriously* thinking about pretending to have a gambling problem in order to crash a session."

That'd be an adventure—and probably not something I could pull off, considering I'd never set foot in a casino. Winstons didn't gamble.

I shook my head. "Nope. If there *is* someone I know attending a session, it might spook him—or her." I leaned forward. "I was thinking you, me, Brandi—stake out."

"Have you thought about what Cal's going to say when he finds out about this little escapade?" Brandi leaned between the passenger's and driver's seats of my extended-cab truck.

It was almost seven, and we'd found a space at the drugstore parking lot in downtown Richardville across the street from Anchor Recovery Center where we had a perfect view of the building's main entrance. Fortunately, the center's parking lot had plenty of lighting because it'd been dark for about an hour.

Ashley twisted around in the passenger's seat to face Brandi. "Are you planning to tattle?"

"No, but he seems to figure stuff out," Brandi said. "I don't want Georgia to blow a chance at happiness because she couldn't keep her nose out of police business."

I fidgeted with the binoculars hanging around my neck. Why hadn't I come on this stakeout alone? "I don't think—"

"Her future happiness isn't wrapped up in Cal Perkins—or any man." Ashley glared at Brandi. "And quit hogging those chips. I haven't had supper."

Brandi tossed the bag of sour cream and onion chips at Ashley. "What's up with you tonight?"

"Low blood sugar." She popped a chip in her mouth.

"This is more than Hangry Ashley," Brandi said.

"Whatever." Ashley's crunching seemed magnified in the small space. "I'm fine."

Brandi's jaw twitched as she crossed her arms. I glanced in the rearview mirror, met her eyes, and shrugged.

There was too much estrogen in this truck. We'd been parked for all of five minutes, and at this point, I was completely convinced that my stepbrothers would've made better sidekicks. "Ladies, could we please focus?"

"My eyes are on the door." Brandi pointed to her eyes and then turned two fingers toward the entrance.

"How long do we have to wait?" Ashley rolled up the chip bag and stuck it on the console.

"According to the schedule, there's only one meeting tonight, so if we stay until a little past seven—in case there're any late-comers—we should be okay." That'd probably be as long as we'd last without killing each other.

There'd been no sign of Olivia, and the only person to arrive was a thin man who'd parked his Honda sedan and jogged to the entrance.

"Speaking of Cal," Brandi said. "Have you figured out what to get him for Christmas?"

I sighed. "Nope."

"I gave her a bunch of suggestions at lunch today, but they didn't help," Ashley said. "It shouldn't be that hard to figure it out, if he's the right guy."

"That's not necessarily true." I ignored the rock thumping down in my gut. "Some people are hard to buy for."

"Hmph." Ashley gazed out the passenger side window. "Has he kissed you yet?"

My face burned. "No."

"Why not?"

"I don't know. I'm not a mind reader." I scowled. "It's probably just because we haven't made our relationship official, and he doesn't like to move too fast." *Or he just doesn't like me.*

"Or it's not right."

I bit my lip and remembered my vow to not think the worst.

The crease in Brandi's forehead deepened. "It's too soon to assume that. It takes time to get to know a person, and there's a lot to be said for not moving too fast."

Thank you, I mouthed into the rearview mirror.

"Have you prayed about all of this?" Brandi asked.

I should've seen that one coming since Brandi believed in praying about everything, but I was thankful she'd changed the subject from the lack of kissing. "No. I asked Kelsey to pray about it." I propped my elbow on the door and leaned my head against my fist. "But I will too."

Lord, help me figure things out with Cal.

The flash of headlights in the recovery center's parking lot caught my attention. I put the binoculars up to my eyes and zeroed in on the white van—with *Litchfield Handyman Services* written on the side.

Olivia's neighbor Pete emerged and plodded toward the entrance. "No wonder his wife was on him about money."

"What?" Brandi asked.

"That guy that just walked in is Olivia Scott's neighbor—Pete Litchfield." I decided to keep the detail about Zach spending the night at Olivia's house to myself. "When I talked to Pete about Olivia disappearing, he didn't mention knowing Zach." However, if Pete knew Zach, that could explain his disgust over Winnie tattling on Zach and Olivia to Pastor Mark.

"He probably wouldn't mention it—if he'd met Zach here," Brandi said.

"True." I passed the binoculars to Ashley, who took a look at two more people walking in.

"Never seen them." She handed them to Brandi.

"Same here." While Brandi was looking, a truck entered the parking lot, but I didn't need the binoculars to recognize the driver who leaped out and strode for the door.

Doug Brockwell.

I remembered Cal's evasiveness when I'd asked about Doug on Saturday night. What if Ruby had been on the right track about Doug but didn't have the story quite right?

Brandi gasped. "No way."

"We shouldn't jump to conclusions," I said as Doug entered the building. Was Doug's gambling problem the source of trouble in his marriage? What if Doug owed some bad guys money, and Zach had been trying to help him and had gotten killed?

"Sure. Best case scenario is that he has a gambling problem." Ashley grabbed the chip bag.

"There might be other explanations." Brandi handed me the binoculars. "What if he's a counselor?"

Brandi. Ever the optimist.

Tap. Tap. Tap.

CHAPTER SEVEN

As the three of us shrieked in unison, I whipped toward the driver's side window. Cal stood outside my truck smirking at us. With my face blazing, I opened the window.

"Evening, ladies. What brings you to Richardville on this fine evening?" His gaze lingered on the binoculars in my hand.

There was no point in even trying to invent a cover story, and the fact that Cal was asking why we were there when it was perfectly obvious, only made me believe he expected me to concoct one.

He was about to be *very* disappointed.

"We're staking out the Anchor Recovery Center to see if anybody related to the case goes in, because it might have something to do with what Zach was trying to tell me. I didn't think it would be a big deal because it's not like I'm crashing a meeting pretending to be addicted to gambling because I don't know a thing about it since Winstons don't gamble except for that one time the Powerball was over a billion and I bought a—"

"Take a breath, Georgia Rae." Cal's dimple had vanished.

Oh boy. The middle name treatment. Only Ashley used my

middle name without being mad at me. Still, I couldn't resist asking another question because, well, Cal was here. "Is Doug Brockwell a suspect in Zach's murder?"

Cal leaned his crossed arms against the open window and gazed at me. "This neighborhood isn't the greatest for three beautiful women to be hanging out in after dark. You should go home. We'll talk later." The stern look in his eyes squashed my desire to argue.

I squirmed. "Yes, sir."

Amusement flickered in his expression as he stepped back. "I'll call you later—*ma'am.*"

I closed the window as I watched him walk toward his car.

"Did you *seriously* call your boyfriend, sir?" Ashley gaped at me. "You aren't even from the South."

"My daddy used sir and ma'am a lot and drilled it into my brother and me—besides, Cal's not my boyfriend—yet."

"You're going to die an old-maid." She shook her head. "*Sir.* Like he pulled us over," she muttered. "No wonder he hasn't kissed you."

I worried about the old-maid thing on a daily basis, so hearing one of my BFFs say it aloud was another kick in the gut.

"Take it easy, Ash." Brandi's teacher voice cut through the cab. "There's no need to discourage Georgia because you're in a rotten mood."

Ashley opened her mouth before snapping it shut and crossing her arms.

The silence ballooned among us. "Let's wait a few more minutes in case someone else we know comes in. Then we can go."

When neither of my friends protested, I assumed it was fine. Five minutes later, we hadn't spotted another familiar face, so I decided we'd had enough fun for one night.

We need to talk. ASAP. In person.

My stomach lurched when I read the text message from Cal later that evening. It was a little past nine, so there was no point in delaying the conversation until tomorrow because there was no way I'd sleep.

Come on over.

I took Gus outside before putting him in his crate and making myself look presentable by changing out of my jammies, brushing my hair, and dabbing on a bit of lip-gloss. In spite of my churning stomach, one thought passed through my ever-so-practical mind.

If Cal dumps me, I won't have to worry about getting him a Christmas gift.

In case anyone ever wondered why I was still single, such thoughts pretty much summed it all up. The doorbell chimed, Gus woofed, and I took a deep breath before opening the door. "Come in."

He followed me past my murder timeline and suspect list on the chalkboard in my dining room and sat on the sofa. "I see you're hard at work on the case."

Gus continued to bark.

Of course he noticed the chalkboard. "I've been spinning a few theories for fun." I joined him on the opposite end of the couch and could hear Ashley mocking me for leaving a buffer.

"You're doing way more than that if tonight's stakeout is any indication."

"We weren't hurting anyone." I drew a throw pillow to my chest as Gus let loose a forlorn howl. I really needed to get him to obedience school.

"What do you plan to do with the information? Confront Doug?" The muscle in his jaw tightened.

"I don't know." Even though I'd known Doug since high school, I wasn't itching to dig into his personal problems.

"Well, let me decide for you. Don't. Do it." Cal's eyes darkened. "He deserves privacy."

"Is he a suspect?"

Gus whined.

"Go let that dog out so we can have this conversation in peace. He doesn't bother me."

I tossed aside the throw pillow and stalked to the utility room. "Bad dog," I hissed as I opened the crate. So much for letting Gus know who was boss. He bounded past me and skidded out of the room in search of my guest.

When I made it to the living room, Gus was resting his paws in Cal's lap while he patted the dog's head.

I sat on the couch. "Is Doug a suspect?"

"He may be involved. Or he may be a man just trying to overcome an addiction. Whatever it is, do you think he wants you poking around in his life?"

I crossed my arms. "Does it matter if he's guilty?" I had trouble believing Doug could've killed Zach. He'd always been kind to me when we were learning choreography during high school show choir. Dancing was never my strength, and though I did eventually learn the moves, it'd always taken me longer than average. I'd felt comfortable dancing with Doug because he wasn't a natural either.

"No. But I'm capable of handling this investigation." He pinched his lips together.

"I know. I trust you."

With a groan, Gus dropped to the floor next to our feet.

"Then what're you doing?"

I drew my knees to my chest. "I want Zach's family to have answers. I want to find Olivia."

"And since you don't trust me to do it, you put yourself—and your friends—in danger."

"It's not like that."

"How is it, Georgia? Imagine my surprise when I stumbled on three beautiful, unarmed women on a stakeout in a less-than-stellar neighborhood. Someone could've hurt you."

"Brandi was packing heat." She always carried a gun—except to school.

A flicker of admiration passed through his expression. "Good."

I bit my lip. "Are you giving me an ultimatum?"

"No." He squeezed the bridge of his nose. "But I care about you and want you to be safe, so please respect me enough to trust me." He stood.

Hearing him say he cared eased my uncertainty about our relationship. But. He'd just played the respect card, and unless I wanted to blow my chance, then I'd better back off because there was nothing more fatal to a relationship than a woman who didn't respect her man.

I might be a relationship novice, but I knew that much.

I got up off the couch and followed him to the front door. "I'll back off. This time I mean it."

"Thank you." He brushed a stray hair out of my eyes. "I don't want anything to happen to you." His tender expression caused my breath to hitch, and my heart thudded as he moved closer.

This is it. He's finally going to kiss me.

Gus wedged himself between us, and I stumbled back, steadying myself against the bench in my foyer. "Sorry." A giggle-gasp hybrid escaped my throat.

"No problem." He ran his fingers through his hair. "I'd better get going."

No! Really, Gus?

He patted the dog's head and kissed my cheek. "Sleep well."

I locked the door behind him, leaned against it, blew out a breath, and looked at my puppy, who gazed up at me with adoring eyes as his tail thumped against the floor.

"We're going to have to have a little talk, buddy."

CHAPTER EIGHT

"I don't know how we're ever going to be ready for the show," Ruby wailed as I walked into the church's greenroom Wednesday afternoon.

"Why?" I tried not to stare at her eyeliner that was at least an eighth of an inch above her lash line. She needed to add a magnifying mirror to her Christmas list.

Too bad I didn't need to get Ruby a present.

She'd woken me up with a phone call at 7:30 and demanded my presence at an emergency meeting. I'd managed to put her off until afternoon because I'd needed to haul grain to the elevator again that morning while prices were still good.

"Drama practice was a *disaster* last night. The angel costume is missing. Doug never showed up. His little Lyla is awful as baby Jesus—can you imagine a sinless baby Jesus with colic?—and the angel can't seem to remember his lines." She put her hands on her face. "How hard can it be to announce the savior's birth? I've never made such awful casting decisions. I have too much going on in my life." She swooned onto the couch. "My judgment is impaired."

Lord, give me strength. "How can I help?" I knew I'd regret those words.

"Will you get my water bottle? Over there." She flicked her fingers toward her paper-strewn desk.

I delivered the water. "Have you thought about recasting baby Jesus?"

Ruby sat up, took a drink, and shook her head so hard her jowls fluttered. "How can you suggest I break the parents' hearts like that? After conveying such an honor on their family? It would crush Doug, and his wife would hate me for all eternity. Besides, I need them to be Mary and Joseph."

As if Doug and his wife didn't have more important issues to deal with at the moment. But Ruby didn't know that, and I wasn't about to spill that secret. "Listen, they might be more understanding than you think. What if you had them use a doll instead of Lyla?"

"We've always had a *real* baby play Jesus." She clutched her water bottle as if her life depended on it. "Unless..."

"What?"

"Would *you* talk to Doug about using a doll?" She put the bottle aside and clasped her hands. "He likes you, so he might accept the decision better coming from you."

Had Jessica Myers found the silver lining in her broken-leg situation? If not, I'd identified it for her—a reprieve from dealing with Ruby.

Nice Georgia. "I can talk to him."

"That'd be wonderful. You don't understand the kind of pressure I'm under right now, and with Zach's death, I'm so burdened. Plus, Carsyn isn't herself lately."

I perched on the couch's arm. "What's wrong?" I should hang out a shingle—Georgia Rae Winston, Personal Therapist. I'd learned a thing or two from the counselor who'd been helping me deal with unresolved issues over my daddy's death.

"She's been hanging around with this new man who's convinced her she doesn't need her Christian faith. My sweet Carsyn's up and rejected everything her daddy and I ever taught her."

"I'm sorry." That information truly was worth her dramatics, but after talking to Carsyn, I had a feeling she'd already been well on her way to rejecting Christianity for a while, and the new man had helped her along. "Where'd she meet this guy?"

"I have no idea. She's freezing me out of her personal life, so I don't know much except he's older. Would you pray for her—for all of us?" Ruby asked.

"Of course." I rested my hand on her shoulder. "I'll find Doug and see what he says about the doll, and then I'll search for the angel costume."

"Oh, thank you. I've been all over the old building looking for that thing, but I must've overlooked it. I don't want to sew another one." She patted my arm. "You're such a blessing to me."

"I'm glad I can help. Now what about the Rob the Angel situation?"

"Rob will learn his lines eventually. He's always been a bit scatterbrained." She sat up. "But his golden good looks are so angelic, I simply don't have it in me to recast him. Plus, we've already ordered a flying harness that fits him."

Rob certainly was hot. Rumor had it a modeling agency had scouted him and offered a contract, but a girl couldn't always believe what she heard. There'd been whispers around town for years that I was going to move to New York City and try to make it on Broadway. I'd nearly snorted coffee out of my nose when Bobbi Sue Miller had asked for confirmation about that gem of a rumor.

I left the greenroom and hustled down the back hall to the equipment room where Doug sat with his feet propped up on his desk. A bulletin board held a picture of his family, as well as a photo of Doug holding up a largemouth bass. A calendar with a picture of a snow-capped mountain hung beside the photo. Red X's marked out dates.

"Hey, Doug." I pointed to the picture. "Nice catch."

"Thanks. Come on in." He dropped his feet to the floor and put his turkey sandwich on his desk next to a bottle of Mountain Dew. "Caught that last summer when I went fishing with my buddy Pete Litchfield."

From Anchor Recovery Center? *Oh sure. Tempt me to ask questions I shouldn't ask.*

"What brings you by?" He stood.

"I'm sorry to interrupt your lunch."

"Naw." He waved a hand.

"Well, um." Why had I let Ruby talk me into this? I tugged my sweatshirt sleeves over my hands. "Ruby has some concerns about how practice went last night—with Lyla."

He chuckled. "Yeah. Ella filled me in. I couldn't make it last night. Is Ruby worried about that too?"

"She's mostly upset about a colicky Baby Jesus."

"I hear you. It's stressing Ella out too." He lowered his voice. "She knows how high-strung Ruby is and was beside herself last night that our little one didn't live up to Ruby's standards."

"How would the two of you feel about using a doll instead?"

"That'd be a huge relief."

"Are you sure?"

"Yes. We've had quite a few challenges lately—enough that I've thought about dropping out of the program. But we made a commitment and didn't want to let the church down. There's already so much upheaval with Zach."

I remembered my promise to Cal. Would I be investigating by asking what was wrong? Or would it be normal Christian caring? It would be weird if I *didn't* ask, right? "Is everything okay?"

"It will be." He studied his hands. "I've made some mistakes, and now I have to be a man and deal with them. I don't want to let Lyla and Ella down."

"Good for you."

He nodded. "Thanks for taking care of this."

"No problem." At least he hadn't offered any details that'd make me feel guilty for breaking my promise to Cal.

"Taking care of what?"

Cal stood in the hall outside of Doug's office.

CHAPTER NINE

"Detective Perkins. What can I do for you?" Doug's forehead creased as he studied Cal. Although Cal wore khaki pants and a button-down shirt instead of a uniform, his imposing presence filled the small room when he stepped through the door.

"I need to ask you some questions," Cal said. "Can you spare a few minutes?"

"Sure." Doug grabbed the Mountain Dew from his desk and took a long swig.

Cal turned to me. "I need to see you in the hall first." He flashed a tight smile at Doug. "I'll be right back."

I waved at Doug. "Catch you later." I actually managed to sound completely nonchalant in spite of my clenching stomach. Drama Queen Ruby would be proud.

Cal motioned for me to go through the door first. "Empty classroom on the left."

His annoyed tone caused my blood pressure to spike as I entered the room.

Cal shut the door and stood in front of it. "What're you doing talking to Doug?"

Aaannnddd there it was. Why did he have to go and assume the worst? I fixed my gaze on the table that held a basket of dry erase markers and a stack of Bibles. I could use wisdom from the good book right about now. I crossed my arms and stared him down. "Taking care of business for the church Christmas program."

"Be specific."

"Why?" I narrowed my eyes. "I am *not* the suspect. Besides, I've known Doug since high school, and if I want to have a conversation with him, I will."

"Unless you're hiding something, it shouldn't be a problem to tell me about the conversation." His jaw twitched.

Hiding something? Was he *seriously* going there? I fought back the naughty words hammering my brain and put my hands on my hips. "You don't trust me to respect your wishes. You don't share about your life or concerns. You've never even asked me over to your apartment." I stepped closer. "I'm expected to spill my secrets and open my life and home, but you give nothing back. Why?"

"Look me in the eyes and tell me you weren't investigating."

Fine. Don't answer my questions. I locked in on his blue eyes. "I wasn't. Investigating."

"Then why won't you tell me what you were talking about?" His face reddened.

"Because I don't want to." I lifted my chin. "It has nothing to do with Zach's murder."

"Fine." He stepped aside and opened the door. "Have a nice day, *Ms.* Winston."

I glared at him. He knew I hated that title. "It's *Miss* Winston."

As I stormed down the hallway to where the new church connected with the old building, my phone rang. When I saw it was Preston, I groaned but decided to answer in spite of my mood. He and Austin had an annoying habit of refusing to leave messages, and they'd keep calling until I picked up.

"Hey, Preston." As soon as I crossed the threshold between the two buildings, a musty smell hit my nostrils.

"Babe! How's it going?"

Ew. It ought to be illegal for stepbrothers to call their stepsisters *babe*. When Dan wasn't around, that's how Preston addressed every woman under age forty—and probably a few over forty.

"Great." *I'm super excited to be having this conversation.*

"Austy's here with me."

"Hi, sissy," Austin said.

Sissy was only slightly better than babe.

"What's going on?" I hurried down the creaky stairs. The basement had a large common room surrounded by classrooms. A piano stood next to a shelf holding the yellow hymn books we'd used when I was a kid.

"Dad and Jill have been talking about getting a tandem bike, so Austin and I thought that you, Dakota, Stella, Mak, and the two of us could go in together and get one for Christmas. Unless you already have a gift. But everybody else is on board, so if you say no, you'll be the family loser."

The morons had come up with a decent idea for once. Though the idea of Mom and Dan zipping around on a tandem bike was puke inducing. "I don't have a gift, so I'm in."

I walked across the room and opened the first of two closets. Since it was empty, except for a few hangers, it was clear Ruby hadn't missed anything.

"Cool. The bikes aren't cheap, and we want to get them the best out there. Otherwise, Dad'll return it."

"Try to find a sale." I opened the other door, revealing a row of our old cream-colored choir robes.

"You'd better come with us, babe," Preston said. "I don't trust us to meet your standards."

I rolled my eyes. "I'm kind of busy and—"

"Do you believe that, Austy? She's trying to ditch us."

"Typical," Austin said.

"What about Dakota?" I began sliding each robe aside, and after I'd passed five or six, I found the angel's tunic.

"Your bro's swamped at work. And Mak's got finals coming up. Nope. It's just us three amigos."

I gritted my teeth and rested my hand on the costume. Why did Dakota get a free pass? It wasn't even tax season yet. "When should I meet you?" Surely, I could endure half an hour with them.

"What're you doing tonight?"

Other than my usual stop at Pizza Heaven for Wednesday Night Wings, I didn't have a good excuse.

"I'll bet she has a date with that cop she's seeing," Austin stage-whispered.

"I'm free tonight." Better to get bike selection over with. I yanked the tunic off the hanger, and the material emitted a floral fabric softener scent.

"Are things not going well with your boyfriend, babe? Do you want to talk to your favorite stepbrothers about it?"

I slammed the closet door. Guys like these Twin Idiots had radar for when they'd be optimally annoying. How else could I possibly explain their lousy timing? "What time. Should I meet you?"

"She's dodging your question, Presty. That's never a good sign."

My blood pressure spiked. They'd better be glad this conversation wasn't taking place in person because I was fairly certain I could've strung them up in a way that'd leave them with a child-less future. "How about seven?" I curled my fingers into a fist but kept my tone light.

"Works for us. Meet us at Silver's Bike Emporium in Richardville."

"Fine. See you tonight." I disconnected, and with a growl, I shoved my phone in my pocket. As I folded the costume over my arm, a faint scratch-scratch sound came from somewhere nearby.

Mice.

I yelped, sprinted for the stairs, and didn't stop running until I was safely in the new building. I leaned against the wall and tried to catch my breath as a childhood memory resurfaced.

Mom had been organizing the church library, which used to be in the basement. I'd been playing in the main room when a mouse had skittered out from behind a trashcan. I'd shrieked and jumped up on a piano bench. Mom had joined me until Pastor Mark had come to our rescue and assured us the coast was clear.

Maybe it was time to tear down the old church after all.

When my breathing and heartrate slowed, I straightened up, marched to the maintenance room, and looked around. "Doug?"

"Right behind you." He trudged through the doorway.

"There are mice in the basement." I held up the angel costume. "I was searching for this when I heard scratching."

"Yeah. We've had trouble with that. I'll set some traps." He took a Mountain Dew can off his desk and tossed it in the trash.

"Thanks." I blew out a breath. "I hate mice. It's the main reason I keep barn cats."

"No problem." His eyes had lost the spark of joy that'd been there earlier.

What had Cal said to him? "Are you okay?"

Doug pressed his lips together. "Yeah. I'll be fine." He couldn't meet my gaze as he fiddled with the strap of his overalls.

Stupid mouse. If it hadn't been for him, I'd have been able to avoid Doug. Now, here he was in front of me. Clearly upset. Besides, if Cal was already assuming the worst of me, I might as well live up to it.

"Does Detective Perkins think you had something to do with Zach's death?"

Doug sighed. "I'm not sure. I've told him everything I know, which isn't much. Still, it freaks me out that he came back with follow-up questions."

I wasn't going to pry about Doug's gambling problem because it was none of my business, but that wouldn't stop me from taking a different approach. "Did Zach ever say anything to you about *anchor*? It was one of his last words."

Doug shoved his hands into his overall pockets and swayed back and forth. "Well, there's an Anchor Recovery Center in Richardville, which is what I told Detective Perkins." He ducked his head. "I've been going to group sessions—since I got in over my head gambling at Hoosier Park—and Zach knew about it, because we were prayer partners."

I had to give him honesty points. "I won't say anything to anybody."

"Thanks."

"For all we know, Zach could've been hallucinating when he said *anchor*. Was anything strange going on with him before he died?"

Doug glanced over his shoulder and then pushed the door shut. "He and Mark kept butting heads," he said quietly. "In fact, the Tuesday before Zach died, he submitted his resignation effective at the end of December, but they were going to wait another week or so to announce it."

My eyes widened. "Who else knew?"

He shook his head. "His family? Olivia since they were dating?"

I remembered what Mona had told me about Pastor Mark

wanting his son-in-law to be the youth pastor. "Did Pastor Mark already have a replacement in mind?"

"Yeah. His son-in-law." Doug grimaced. "Thanksgiving Day, I got a notification on my phone about a problem with the church's furnace, so I stopped by to check it around five or so. Mark was in here showing Dax around like it was a given he'd be hired for Zach's job."

"Did they see you?"

"Naw."

I thought of the phone call Carsyn had overheard at Solid Rock. "Did you call Zach and tell him?"

Doug lifted his chin. "Sure did. It ticked him off, but he showed up for work the next day like nothing had happened." He gazed down at his boots. "I still feel terrible that I left to buy that extension cord for the nativity scene. If I'd been there, we could've gotten him to the hospital sooner, and he wouldn't have..."

I rested my hand on Doug's shoulder. "Don't beat yourself up. There's no way you could've known."

He nodded, and tears filled his eyes.

At least I hoped there was no way he'd known.

That night, I stopped at Pizza Heaven for the Wednesday Night Wings special—something I did on an embarrassingly regular basis. Driving out of downtown Wildcat Springs on my way to Silver's Bike Emporium, I fought an aching throat as I thought about Cal. Why hadn't I told him what he wanted to know about Doug? Why had I felt the need to cause an argument?

I stopped at the town's single traffic light at Main and Pearl Streets and drummed my fingers against the steering wheel.

Why couldn't he trust me? Not with the case. I understood

he couldn't talk about it. No, he was holding something back in his personal life.

The light blinked green, and I drove through the intersection and followed the highway to Richardville. I wasn't good at this whole relationship thing. God had probably been doing me a favor by leaving me single for all these years.

I pressed play on the navigation screen and sang along to Chanticleer's version of "Ave Maria."

When I was about halfway to Richardville, blinding headlights drew my attention to my rearview mirror, and I scowled. The white SUV that had been following me since I pulled out of the public parking lot in downtown Wildcat Springs zoomed closer.

I stifled a few choice words. "You are *not* going to drive my truck, jerk!" I glared in the mirror, even though darkness concealed me.

When Daddy taught me to drive, he'd been fond of telling me to never let the person behind me manipulate me into exceeding the speed limit.

I let off the accelerator and hoped the driver would pass. Instead, the SUV slowed to match my speed—and took the tailgating to a whole new level. Since I was about five minutes from the bike shop, which was in downtown Richardville, I made a quick right into a subdivision to take the back way.

The SUV followed through the winding streets.

As I exited the subdivision, I blew through a yellow light, but the vehicle kept pace. I took another left past a gas station and Solid Rock Mission. I hung a right next to the public library, but the SUV remained inches from my bumper.

Now there was no question this was deliberate.

Tightening my grip, I pressed the voice command button on my steering wheel. "Call Preston cell."

"Calling Preston on cell," the navigation system's female voice said.

The phone rang twice. "Babe! Don't tell me you're running late."

"Are you at the bike shop?"

"Yes."

"We aren't getting any younger, sissy," Austin chimed in.

"Shut up. This is important." I gritted my teeth. "I'm driving south on Webster Street approaching the shop. A white SUV's been tailing me for miles, and I can't lose it. When I pull in, I need you to take a picture of the SUV's license plate as it passes and send it to me."

Preston and Austin both emitted low chuckles. "You need us as sidekicks," they said in unison. I pictured the two of them gleefully bumping chests.

Life Lesson #41: God has a sense of humor, and he knows how to use it.

I rolled my eyes. "Yes. I need you." I glanced in the rearview mirror and tightened my grip on the wheel. *Still there.* "I'm not joking. Please come through for me."

"We've got your back, babe." Preston disconnected.

I blew out a breath. The bike shop was coming up on the left, so I slowed the truck's speed. Austin and Preston stood on the sidewalk under a streetlight, with their phones outstretched.

At the last second, I turned into the half-empty parking lot. The SUV swerved around me, and the tires squealed as it roared away. I parked next to Preston's Mustang—his baby—and, clutching my purse, I hopped out of my truck. "Did you get it?"

They jogged over. "Sure did, sissy." Austin held up his phone.

Sissy. So, that means Austin's the one in the gray overcoat. My phone vibrated, so I took it out of my purse and studied the picture. The plate number was completely clear. "Good work."

Austin staggered backward. "It's a miracle. An actual, real-life compliment from Georgia Winston."

I snorted. "An actual, real-life situation where you *deserved* a compliment from Georgia Winston."

Preston grinned. "One more coming your way."

I opened the picture. Preston had managed to get a shot of the driver—who was wearing a black ski mask. "Way to go above and beyond."

"You're welcome. Now maybe you'll see how valuable Austin and I are."

That was a big maybe, but I didn't feel like contradicting him at the moment. With shaking fingers, I texted Cal the pictures.

Not investigating. Minding own business when white SUV tailgated me from Wildcat Springs to bike shop in Richardville. Stepbrothers took pic of plate number and driver.

I sent the message, shut my phone down, and dropped it in my purse since I couldn't deal with a reprimand from Cal right now.

"Seriously. Why was creepy ski-mask guy following you?" Preston crossed his arms. For once, my stepbrother's voice held no mockery—only sincerity.

I blew out a breath. "Last Friday I found one of my church's pastors after he'd been poisoned, and he might've been trying to tell me something important before he died."

"Whoa. Two dead bodies," Austin said. "We should stay away from her." He glanced at his brother.

"Thanks." I rolled my eyes. "And technically, it's one dead body. Zach died at the hospital."

"What'd he say before he died?" Preston asked.

"Anchor."

Austin raised his eyebrows. "That's it?"

"Yep. He might've been hallucinating."

Preston looked over his shoulder in the direction that the SUV had fled. "The person who killed him doesn't know that."

"Right." They weren't half bad at this sidekick gig.

"Which could be why they're coming after you." Austin's eyes widened, and he elbowed his brother. "Dude, it's like a movie."

"Why tailgate me?" I gnawed my lip as I looked back and forth at them. "There are more explicit ways to warn someone to back off."

I'd experienced one or two in my time.

"Unless the perp planned to run you off the road." Preston looked at his brother, and understanding dawned in their wide-eyed expressions.

"To make it look like an accident," they said in unison.

It didn't seem that farfetched. After all, half of Wildcat Springs knew I went to Pizza Heaven for wings most Wednesday nights. I needed to do a better job of shaking up my routine.

Austin bristled. "Don't worry. We'll protect you."

"Like we would Mak." Preston threw his arm over my shoulder. "We're family—whether you like it or not."

"Thanks." I shivered, shoved my hands into my coat pockets, and glanced toward the bike shop. "Let's get inside."

We hustled toward the brick building. In the window, a bike covered in multi-colored Christmas lights gave off a friendly glow. A woman with waist-length hair greeted us and led us to the tandem bikes in the back of the store, where she left us to weigh our options.

I didn't know about my stepbrothers, but I was having trouble concentrating. The three choices of tandem bikes seemed the same to me except for differences in color.

After a couple of minutes of studying the signs, Preston

sighed. "These are nice, but I don't think Dad'll go for any of them."

"I vote we keep shopping," Austin said. "Georgia?"

"Fine. Whatever you think." My voice sounded far away. If I hadn't taken a shortcut through the subdivision, how far would the driver have taken things?

In a daze, I followed Preston and Austin out of the shop and out to our vehicles.

"Have you heard back from your boyfriend about those pictures?" Austin stopped next to the Mustang's trunk.

"No. I shut my phone off. I don't need him chewing me out." As soon as the words slipped out, I wanted to shove them back in my mouth.

"Why would he do that?" There was no mistaking the protective edge in Austin's voice.

Smooth, Georgia Rae. I sighed and explained about Cal misunderstanding my conversation with Doug Brockwell earlier in the day.

My stepbrothers exchanged glances. "If he blows it with you, he's an idiot," Preston said.

I studied Preston's expression. Again—not even a hint of mockery. "That's officially the nicest thing you've ever said to me."

"Yep. I'm just that kind of guy."

Austin narrowed his eyes. "I'll take him on if you want." In spite of his pretty boy looks, he'd been an offensive lineman on Richardville High School's football team, and Preston had played defense.

"Thanks." I smothered a giggle as I unlocked my truck and opened the door. "Cal and I will figure things out."

"Okay." There was no mistaking the flicker of disappointment in Austin's expression. "We'll look for other bike options and let you know."

"Great." I climbed in the truck.

"We're following you home." Preston shut my door before I could protest.

I waved and started the engine. As much as it pained me to admit it, my stepbrothers weren't so bad after all.

CHAPTER TEN

W hen I arrived home, Cal was waiting in the driveway. Before I could even pull into the garage, Preston and Austin had hopped out of the Mustang and were hulking toward him. He'd been leaning against his car and whistling but straightened up when he realized the twins meant business.

I jumped out of my truck and waved my arms. "Guys, that's Cal."

They didn't slow down. I raced over as Preston extended his hand. "Preston Farthing. This is Austin. We're here to make sure Georgia's okay." He squared his shoulders as he and Cal shook.

"Got to look out for family." Austin crossed his arms and gave Cal the once-over.

Cal looked back and forth between them. "Sounds like she needs it."

Thanks a lot. But after tonight, how could I disagree?

Cal cleared his throat. "I ran the plate number you sent me."

"And?" I asked.

My orange cat trotted over from his home in the barn to investigate and rub his head against my legs.

"The SUV belongs to a seventy-six-year-old woman who's been in the rehab hospital recovering from a broken hip for the past three weeks. Didn't even know her vehicle was missing. Neither did her kids." He surveyed Austin and Preston. "Good work on the pictures."

They puffed out their chests. "Thanks."

I pointed to the door. "You're all welcome to come in."

"Thanks, but we'd better get home," Preston said. "Take care."

"Yeah, we'll leave you alone to make up." Austin made a kissing noise before sauntering to Preston's car.

I longed for a crater to open up in my driveway, so I could disappear into oblivion. Instead, I bent down and petted the cat's head.

Cal chuckled as they zoomed away. "You told them we had a fight?"

I stood and crossed my arms. "I may've let it slip that we had a disagreement. That's why they were ready to jump you. I'm sorry."

"I'm glad they were looking out for you." His eyes twinkled.

"Now they think they're my sidekicks for life."

"If you don't investigate, you won't need sidekicks." He smirked.

I opened my mouth to protest but snapped it shut. "Do you want to come in?"

"I need to make sure everything's okay," he said.

"I have a security system."

"Humor me."

"Okay."

We headed inside, where I disabled the system, and Cal checked every room in my house while I tended to Gus.

When he finished, he came into the kitchen. "Everything's fine. Sorry I was hard on you earlier today. Doug told me you were asking him about using a doll for baby Jesus. I should've trusted you." Cal met my eyes, and sincerity shone from his gaze.

"Thank you. I accept your apology, and I'm sorry I didn't tell you why I was talking to him in the first place." I ducked my head. "But I have a confession."

"What?" A slight edge returned to his tone.

"I didn't ask Doug anything about the case when you saw me, but later, I had to find him after I heard a mouse in the church basement. He looked upset, so since you were already mad at me, I asked him about Zach—and the word *anchor*." I held up both hands. "I didn't confront him about gambling, but he told me about Anchor Recovery Center anyway."

"You've known him for years. If he wanted to tell you, that's his business." He didn't sound thrilled, but he clearly wasn't as upset as he'd been earlier.

"He wouldn't have had to admit it. We talked about Zach resigning because he didn't get along with Pastor Mark."

"You'd have heard about that sooner or later." He laced his fingers through mine and pulled me closer. "I thought about the stuff you said—about me holding back."

"And?" I rested my hand on his chest.

"I'll cook dinner at my place if you're free tomorrow night at seven. Does that work?"

I met his eyes. "That's perfect." Finally. I'd get to see his apartment.

He lowered his head.

Buzzz. Buzzz.

Cal stepped back. "Sorry." He pulled his phone out of his pocket and glanced at it. "My sister. She got LEGO sets for her kids." He turned it toward me so I could see the pictures.

"Those are cute." Seriously? Was she in cahoots with Gus?

"I'll see you tomorrow." He shoved his phone back in his

pocket and then gave me a pleading, little-boy look. "Don't forget I could use some help with Christmas decorating."

Cal lived in an apartment above an older gentleman's garage on Park Street. A barren tree stretched its branches downward over the roof as if it were keeping a protective hand over the building.

I clutched a bag full of ornaments that I'd purchased earlier that day at Crafter's Paradise in Richardville, climbed the wooden staircase on the side of the building, and knocked on the door.

Cal was whistling "Jingle Bell Rock" as he opened the door. He wore a green camouflage-print apron. "Come on in. Dinner's almost ready."

"Wait. I hear you, but I can't see you." I reached out and patted his apron.

He laughed.

"Love the camo print." I hugged him.

"Thanks." He smiled.

Would I ever get tired of seeing his dimple? I hoped not.

I held out the bag. "Christmas cheer. I picked some baseball-themed ornaments along with more traditional ones."

"Cool." He set the bag on the counter and headed for the stove.

Yellow floral paper adorned the walls, and brown appliances from the 1960s or 70s completed the retro look. Strange that Cal couldn't afford a better apartment since he'd played professional baseball when he was younger. But there probably weren't that many places to rent in Wildcat Springs.

He motioned to the stove. "It's ancient, but it gets the job done. I'm looking to buy my own place in the country—just haven't found the right one."

"They can be hard to come by." I kept my tone light, but my face burned at the thought that if our relationship progressed to marriage, he wouldn't need to buy his own place. But once again, I was getting *way* ahead of myself—especially since we were both acting kind of awkward.

"Have a seat." He motioned toward the dented and scratched table. There weren't any personal touches in his kitchen to help me figure out what he might like for a gift.

Once I was settled, Cal set a plate containing a pork chop with an apple topping, grits, and green beans in front of me.

"This looks great." I placed a napkin in my lap.

He sat down with his own plate. "Let's pray." He clasped my hand and said a quick blessing for our food.

I took a bite of the tender pork chop, thankful that I had something to do. "Oh. My word. This is fabulous."

Life Lesson #24: Try to snag a man who can cook.

"Thanks. I learned to love grits when I played ball in Texas. One of my buddies was a native and taught me the right way to cook 'em." He didn't start eating right away—long enough to get me wondering if I'd managed to smear grits all over my face.

I wiped my mouth. "You okay?"

"You were right. I've been holding out on you."

I wasn't sure I liked the sound of that. I clutched my napkin as if it were the edge of a cliff. "How so?"

"My parents are getting a divorce."

I loosened my grip. "I'm so sorry."

"Thirty-seven years of marriage—down the drain." He put his fork down and scrubbed his hand over his face. "My mom up and decided she's not happy with my dad, and her new boy toy would make her life great."

No wonder he'd been holding back with me. Watching a marriage disintegrate was enough to make anyone cautious about relationships. "When did you find out?"

"Last month. I went to Cleveland for Thanksgiving, because my sister and I thought we could help cheer Dad up." He shook his head. "He announced at dinner that he's moving to Florida in a couple of weeks to be closer to some woman he met online."

"Yikes."

"Yeah. He wouldn't listen when I told him rebounding was a bad idea. He insisted Florida had always been part of his retirement plan, even though I've never heard about it. He swears he isn't going to let the divorce stop him. Never mind that he's always made fun of retirees who can't hack Ohio winters and escape to Florida every year."

"Did you see your mom?"

His eyes darkened. "No. I still need some time, so I don't say something I'll have to apologize for." He took a drink of water. "The worst part is, Danielle and I didn't see the split coming. Mom and Dad were so good at hiding their problems that we believed they were happy. All my years in law enforcement should've taught me that people aren't always what they seem, but I had a huge blind spot when it came to my family."

"I'm sorry."

"Danielle's taking it a lot harder than me. Mom always helped her with the kids, but ever since she started her affair, she's been too busy with her boyfriend, who's like fifteen years younger. Now with Dad leaving..." He cut a piece of meat. "So that's what I've been dealing with." He took a bite of pork chop.

"I'm sorry I was so hard on you."

"No, you're right. If we're going to get to know each other, then you need to know what's happening in my life. But I expect the same from you."

"Deal." I clasped his hand. "I don't think there's anything else I haven't told you."

"Good." He squeezed my hand.

We enjoyed our food for a few minutes.

"Let me ask you something." He cut a piece of meat. "You're going to be spending a lot of time at the church during the next week because of rehearsals, right?"

"Yep."

"Keep an eye on everyone. You're a natural at getting people to open up, so if you hear or learn anything—and I do mean *anything*—that you think might be important, tell me."

"You're bringing me into the investigation?" I tried to keep excitement from spilling into my voice but didn't quite manage.

"Sort of. If you want to think of it that way. Just tell me what you find out, and don't go off on any wild goose chases by yourself."

"Should I pay attention to anyone in particular?"

He cocked an eyebrow. "Nope."

That I could do. "Why the change of heart?"

"Your adventure on the way to the bike store tells me you're probably involved whether you want to be or not. We might as well roll with it."

"Is Detective Kimball okay with it?" I couldn't bring myself to call him Marvin.

"Yeah. After I told him about the SUV tailgating you, he agreed that you're right in the middle of this, so we should use that to our advantage—since you've given us some solid tips in the past." Cal pointed to my plate. "You want more?"

Yes. "No, thank you. It was delicious. Let me help you clean up."

"Sure." He grinned. "Then we can decorate before we have some strawberry cheesecake."

Strawberry cheesecake? He was definitely my dream man.

CHAPTER ELEVEN

The next morning, I tried to forget the fact that Cal still hadn't kissed me the night before as I chugged my Moon Landing Mocha on the way to church to have a vocal rehearsal with Sharon Anderson, who was playing Millie the Time-Traveling Scientist.

What was I doing wrong?

We'd had a blast decorating his Christmas tree, and Cal had played Christmas music and whistled as I sang. At the end of the evening, he'd given me a hug, thanked me for helping him decorate, and sent me on my way. Gus hadn't even been there to interrupt. No text messages disturbed us. Maybe Cal unloading his family problems had killed the mood.

I pulled into the church parking lot, found a space close to the door, and strode to the entrance.

Even with the visit to Cal's apartment, I still wasn't any closer to figuring out a gift for him. He had a few pictures of family sitting on his entertainment center cabinet, but that was it for personal touches.

I walked into the church office. "Good morning, Mona!"

"Morning." She set her coffee mug on her desk. "Sharon called and said she's running a few minutes late."

I shrugged and took another sip of mocha. "No problem."

A petite, fifty-something woman carrying a box emerged from the back hallway. "This is the last load. I left most of the books on his shelf. I'd like to donate them to your church library."

"Thank you," Mona said. "I'll be happy to move them for you."

As the woman drew closer, I saw the resemblance.

"You're Zach's mother?" I asked.

"Yes—Elaine Mishler."

"Georgia Winston." I put my coffee cup on the counter. "I'm very sorry for your loss."

Elaine studied me and set the box down at her feet. "You're the one who tried to save my son."

"Yes, ma'am." I clasped her hand. "I'm sorry it wasn't enough."

Tears filled her eyes. "Did he know what was happening?" She squeezed my hand before letting go.

What could I say? The brutal truth was Zach had been in horrible shape when I'd found him. "He didn't have much strength left. He said *anchor* as if it were important. I thought he meant Jesus was his anchor, but when I said that, he corrected me. Does that word mean something to you?"

"I wish it did." Her chin trembled. "I should've known if something bad was happening in my own son's life, but I didn't. He was always a good boy—kind and thoughtful. I couldn't even give the detectives a reason someone would've given him poisoned tea leaves."

I gaped at her as I absorbed what she'd said. "Someone poisoned the tea *before* he made it."

"The killer mixed Jimsonweed seeds into the blend." Tears filled her eyes. "If I hadn't taught him to love all kinds of tea, this wouldn't have happened." She grabbed a tissue from her pocket and dabbed her eyes. "I know it's not my fault, but still..."

"Do the police know where the tea came from?"

"If they do, they haven't told me, but obviously it came from someone he trusted—who knew he liked peppermint-flavored tea."

Someone like Olivia Scott—or anyone on the church staff.

Elaine removed her keys from her pocket. "I'd better go. I have to finish packing his apartment before heading back to Michigan for his memorial service."

I hugged her. "I'm praying for you and your family."

"Thank you." Elaine picked up the box.

I followed her to the door, opened it, and returned to Mona's desk. "I feel terrible for Mrs. Mishler."

"I can't imagine losing my child—let alone to murder." She fidgeted with the fringe on her black sweater. "Jimsonweed is awful. I heard about a teenager who died from trying to get high on the stuff last summer."

"Do you know who?"

"No. I heard it from another mom when I was taking a cycling class at Fitness Universe. She didn't mention names, but she was warning the rest of us parents." Mona brushed her bangs off her forehead, and my eyes fell on her left ring finger that displayed a huge princess-cut diamond.

Thankful for the opportunity to change the subject, I pointed to the ring. "Nice rock. Do you have some news?"

She sat up straighter and blushed. "It happened fast, but Jim is everything I could want in a guy, and he loves my kids. They think he's pretty cool too. His daughter Mia is sixteen and gets along great with Leah."

"Congratulations."

"Thanks."

"Tell me about him."

"He's the director at Solid Rock Mission, and he has a heart for the less fortunate."

"Jim Phillips?"

She brightened. "You know him?"

"We've met." Interesting that he'd be able to afford such a big ring on a mission director's salary. But it could be a family heirloom. "How'd you get together?"

"His brother Tristan is my landlord, so he introduced us."

A blast of cold air tickled the back of my neck, and I faced Sharon.

She pushed her gray, windblown hair out of her eyes. "I'm *sooo* sorry. I slept through my alarm."

"No worries." Her timing couldn't have been more perfect. "Let's get started."

"I met Zach Mishler's mom at church, and she told me about the poisonous seeds in the tea blend." I said to Cal that evening as I tossed a doggie biscuit into Gus's crate. He scampered in, and I shut the door.

"Yep," he said. "Nasty stuff. The whole Jimsonweed plant is poisonous."

"I read about it." That afternoon, I'd done a quick Google search, and I'd learned that the flowering plant grew in Indiana during warm months, but the seeds could be purchased online year-round. "Any ideas on who gave him the tea?"

"We have a strong lead." For having been dating just a month, I was getting pretty good at recognizing his I-Can't-Tell-You-That look. He squinted, just slightly, and his eyes twinkled, but he pressed his lips together, as if he were trying to look like he disapproved.

"Good. I'm thinking it's not anyone on the church staff, or you wouldn't have encouraged me to be on the lookout for you."

"Nothing is certain yet."

Gus started whining, so Cal and I made a quick exit. He was taking me to Wildcat Lanes, which was bound to be interesting. I hadn't bowled for probably ten years. He opened the passenger door of the Jeep that he drove when he wasn't working, and I hopped in.

When we were on our way, I couldn't resist another question. "Do you know anything about a teenager dying from Jimsonweed last summer?"

He drove toward the highway. "No. Who told you that?"

"Mona. But she didn't know who the kid was. She heard it from another mom when she was working out."

"Good to know." Cal scrubbed his hand over his chin.

When we arrived at the bowling alley about twenty minutes later, nearly all of the lanes were filled. Though no one had smoked inside for at least ten years, the smell of stale cigarette smoke lingered and mixed with grease from the concession stand. After Cal paid for a couple of games and we got our shoes, we found our lane.

Please, God, don't let me embarrass myself. I kicked off my silver sneakers and put on the worn bowling shoes.

The chorus of falling pins followed by a cheer drew my attention to the lane next to us. Ella Brockwell did a victory shimmy before high-fiving her husband Doug. When she met my gaze, she waved. "First strike of the night."

Doug's eyes shined. "She's a tough one."

I laughed. "I'm hoping I don't bowl all gutter balls."

"We can always put up the bumpers." Cal looked up from the console where he was entering our initials.

"Nope." I lifted my chin. "I'm good."

Doug picked up a ball from the return. "You two have fun."

He winked and approached the lane. He let the ball fly, and a few seconds later—strike. He pumped his fist, and Ella giggled.

It was nice to see them getting along.

"Ladies first." Cal motioned toward the lane and rested his hand on the small of my back.

I bit my lip and selected a burgundy-marbled ball from the return. At least it was pretty. Taking a deep breath, I approached my lane and drew the ball back.

Nice and easy.

As I swung through, the ball collided with the back of my leg. My knee buckled, and the ball plunked out of my hand. While I limped backward, trying not to shriek in pain, the ball rolled about halfway down the lane before it dribbled left and died in the gutter.

Cal hopped up. "Are you all right?"

"Yeah." I rubbed my leg and glanced around to see if anyone else—especially Doug and Ella—had seen. But they were—thankfully—focused on each other. "I'll probably have a gigantic bruise tomorrow, but I'm tough. I'm sorry I embarrassed you by looking like such a klutz and—"

"Relax." He rested a hand on my shoulder. "You didn't embarrass me." A reassuring smile spread over his face.

"Okay." I tried to forget about his dimple as I picked up the ball from the return. "I'll be more careful."

"You've got this."

Jaw clenched, I marched forward. This time, I eased up on my follow through and managed to miss my leg. The ball sailed straight down the middle of the lane, and I crossed my fingers.

Please, please, please don't fall in the gutter.

The ball cracked against the pins, knocking seven of them down.

I blew out the breath I'd been holding. At least I wouldn't have a night of *all* gutter balls.

Cal stood. "Good job."

I dropped down on the bench and watched him bowl a strike —with ease.

Be still my heart. I clapped. "Way to go."

A little bit later, and without further embarrassing incidents, Cal had just won our first game when my phone rang. "This is Georgia."

"Ms. Winston, this is Safe Home calling to inform you that your security system alarm has been triggered. Shall we notify the police?"

My eyes widened, and my heart chugged. "Yes. I'm not home." I didn't care about my stuff, but if someone hurt Gus...

Cal turned, concern filling his expression.

"We'll take care of that right away."

"Thank you." I disconnected and stood. "Someone's breaking into my house."

CHAPTER TWELVE

My place was trashed. By the time the sheriff's department had been able to respond, the perps had fled, leaving overturned furniture, spilled drawers, and broken glass from my back door in their wake.

Gus had been howling in his cage, but thankfully, he was fine.

My laptop was gone, yet my TV, DVD player, and jewelry were intact.

"Are you missing any cash or other valuables?" Cal asked after I'd wandered around in a daze trying to remember everything I owned. Gus didn't leave our sides.

"I need to check the safe." I bolted out of the office and into the hallway where I opened the basement door, and we descended into the basement's musty depths.

I didn't have the fancy walkout kind, complete with a pool table, home theater, and wet bar. Nope. Mine was the one-hundred-year-old variety that I used for storage and for shelter during the tornado warnings that were all-too-frequent here in the good ol' heartland.

Daddy'd built a safe room years ago in the corner, and it contained an actual safe and was large enough to duck into during storms.

Cal waited outside the tiny room. I opened the safe and inspected the contents while Gus sat at my feet. My wad of emergency cash was in place, and so was my birth certificate, passport, and other important papers. I secured the door and came out.

"Everything's here, but I'm not surprised since they obviously didn't have time to make it down here." I shook my head as we tromped back upstairs. "Why would they take my laptop but not the other electronics?"

I entered my office, which contained the worst of the mess. Papers from my filing cabinets blanketed the floor, and Gus walked around, nudging them with his nose. It'd take me weeks to reorganize my farm files, and my tax prep would be even more arduous than normal. The dog finished sniffing the room, dropped down in the doorway, and kept guard.

Cal ran his hand through his hair. "A laptop is easy to carry away."

"Yeah. And fairly new." I'd bought it about two years ago. I shifted and pointed to the upended drawers. "It's like they were looking for something in particular."

"Such as?"

I sighed. "I know this is going to sound crazy, but with that stolen SUV tailgating me the other night, it's like Zach's killer thinks I know something—or have evidence of some kind. Except I don't."

"Because word's gotten out that he spoke to you before he died."

"Yeah. Which is my own fault since I went around asking questions and telling people he said *anchor*." I held up my hands in surrender. "But Jimsonweed can cause hallucinations, so he was probably babbling about nothing."

"That's very likely."

I crossed my arms. "They'd really know I didn't have anything if they got a look at my chalkboard in the dining room." My mind whirred with all the details I'd learned. "There's one good bit of news."

"What?" Cal furrowed his brow.

"We can eliminate Doug as a suspect since he and his wife were with us at the bowling alley."

"Maybe. Unless he's part of a conspiracy." He glanced at the mess. "But you're probably right. How about I help you secure your back door and straighten this up, and then you can tell me if there's anything else missing."

"Thanks." I batted my eyes—just a little. "You're the best."

Saturday morning, Ashley, Brandi, and I met at Latte Conspiracies for breakfast. The chatter from the Saturday morning crowd echoed against the exposed ceilings, and since I got my food first, I claimed an empty booth in the corner before someone beat me to it.

While I waited for my friends to get to the table, I picked at a blueberry scone. I wasn't looking forward to bringing up the break-in at my house because I didn't want a safety lecture—though they'd mean well.

"I'm sorry for how I acted the other night during our stakeout." Ashley set an oversized coffee mug and a plate with a cranberry orange muffin on the table and sank into the booth.

"You're forgiven," I said.

Holding a plate with a cherry Danish, Brandi slid in next to me. "We all have off days. It's okay."

"No, it's not." Ashley dug into her handbag, withdrew two

boxes wrapped in red-striped paper, and slid them across the table. "Peace offering."

Brandi and I exchanged glances before we opened the gifts and giggled. "Mistletoe." I held up the artificial sprigs adorned with white berries and a red bow.

Ashley's brown eyes gleamed. "Make sure you hang that right where Cal will walk."

"You can bet I will." Even after helping me straighten my office the night before, he *still* hadn't kissed me, but to be fair, the mood hadn't exactly been romantic. "Thanks." I stashed the box in my purse before anyone else saw us and started telling everything they knew.

"I'm thinking the opening between your foyer and living room," Brandi said. "Hang it low, so he doesn't miss it."

"Good call." Ashley winked and turned to Brandi. "Where are you planning on putting yours, hon?"

"It'll be perfect between my dining room and kitchen." She rested a hand on Ashley's arm. "Thank you."

"You're welcome. Anything you want to tell us about your love life?"

Brandi bit a hangnail and looked at me. "I went on a date last night with Jon."

I leaned forward. "How'd it go?" Though I hadn't hit it off with Jon Nordmeyer, I suspected he might have more in common with my friend and had suggested they get to know each other.

"He took me to dinner at Salvador's," Brandi said. "He's a nice guy, and we had a lot to talk about."

"Will there be a second date?" Ashley asked.

"If he asks, I'll go again since we had fun. He has a lot of great qualities."

That wasn't a glowing endorsement, and her tone indicated she was trying to convince herself, but it was progress from not dating at all. "I'm glad he didn't scare you away."

"Me too." Brandi popped a bit of Danish in her mouth.

I took a drink of coffee and debated bringing up the break-in.

Ashley peeled the wrapper off her muffin. "So, heads up. I have to cancel Bible study tomorrow."

"What's going on?" Brandi asked.

Ashley pinched off a ladylike bite and shook her head. "Something came up."

Brandi's forehead creased. "Do you want me to host? I'd be happy to."

I was glad Brandi had stepped up and taken that hint. Though I took my turn on a regular basis, hospitality wasn't exactly my gift. Not to mention I didn't feel like embarking on a last-minute cleaning frenzy when I still had files to put in order.

Ashley swallowed. "If you want." She dabbed her lips with her napkin.

Brandi picked up her phone. "If you're sure, I'll text everyone now."

"Whatev." Ashley shrugged. "It's totally up to you."

The glimmer of Normal Ashley had vanished. "Will you be able to come to Brandi's?"

"Maybe. No promises." She drank her coffee.

"You know you can tell us if something's going on." Brandi looked up from her phone.

"Absolutely." I took a bite of scone.

A flash of pain flickered in her eyes. "Thanks." Ashley eyed me over the rim of her coffee mug. "Have you figured out what to get Cal for Christmas?"

I swallowed. "Nope. I'll think of something." In spite of the lack of kissing, I was feeling more confident about our relationship in general since he'd opened up to me about his family.

"You could get a tandem bike." Ashley smirked. "I'll bet Austin and Preston would be thrilled to help you pick it out."

Brandi giggled.

"Real funny." But I laughed anyway. "Since I don't want you hearing it from someone else, you should know my house was broken into last night while Cal and I were bowling."

Brandi set her coffee mug on the table, and Ashley's eyes widened as I filled them in on the details.

"The only thing missing was your computer?" Ashley asked when I finished.

"Yeah."

"Do you need help cleaning up?" Brandi asked.

"No—but thank you. I have to reorganize my files."

Brandi patted her purse. "If you need help buying a gun, I know a guy."

Considering a security system and a dog hadn't discouraged robbers, purchasing a firearm might not be a bad idea, so I needed to get over my negative feelings about guns. Still, I wasn't comfortable with the idea of toting one around. "I'll think about it."

Saturday afternoon, armed with a red, glitter-covered poinsettia, I paid a visit to Beverly Alspaugh, who lived down the road from me. As soon as I rang the doorbell, a yippy bark responded. The front door swung open, and Beverly's face lit up. Instead of the curly gray wig she wore in public, a scarf covered her head.

"Good to see you, dearie."

"Do you feel like company?"

"Absolutely." She stepped aside, and her dog, a black Schnauzer named Miss Peacock, sniffed my leg as I entered. No doubt she got a good whiff of Gus. "I didn't sleep well last night, but I got some extra rest this morning. I've been feeling better lately."

"That's wonderful." I handed her the flower.

"How pretty. Thank you!" She set it on the credenza near the door. "Come have a seat."

We entered the living room, and her dog sat at her feet. A ceramic Christmas tree with multicolored lights rested on top of her old-fashioned cabinet TV. A nativity scene on the mantle completed Beverly's decorations.

"I just got some good news. My cancer's in remission." She tugged her cardigan closed, as if to stave off a chill in the toasty room. "Only the Lord knows how long, but I'll take it."

"Beverly, that's wonderful. Thank the Lord!"

She rocked back and forth in her recliner. "How are things with my great-nephew?"

"Progressing." I wasn't sure how much to say. It'd been Beverly's idea for Cal and me to meet, though we'd encountered each other before she'd had a chance to fix us up.

"You'd like them to progress more quickly?"

"Not necessarily." I folded my hands and rested them in my lap. "It's just that...I wish I knew him better, so I'd know what to get him for Christmas. I asked what he wanted, and he said he didn't need anything. I want it to be special, but not too special. We haven't been dating that long, and I don't want to set the bar too high or seem too serious or have my gift inadvertently put pressure on him—"

"Relax, Georgia."

Even Miss Peacock lifted her head and panted, as if to reassure me. Though she was probably trying to cool herself because the house was at least eighty degrees. I pushed up my sweater sleeves. "I'm sorry for babbling."

She chuckled. "It's okay." Beverly rocked some more. "Perhaps you shouldn't worry about what to buy, since gifts aren't all that important to him. Try to figure out how he wants to be loved and go from there."

How he wanted to be loved. That would definitely take some more digging.

Sunday night at Brandi's house, I slathered icing on a bell-shaped cookie and dumped red and green sprinkles on it before taking a bite. She'd set up a decorate-your-own-cookie bar in her kitchen, and our Bible study group huddled around her island putting festive touches on the homemade sugar cookies. Tonight's gathering included J.T., Brandi, Evan, and engaged couple Dave and Heather.

Ashley had failed to give a reason for her absence.

"How many more days of school until break?" I asked Evan as I broke the top off my cookie and popped it in my mouth.

"Thirteen." He squirted some yellow icing on a star. "Cal still wouldn't come with you?" He placed his cookie on a napkin and headed for Brandi's living room.

I followed, giving the mistletoe hanging from the opening a wide berth. "No."

I didn't want to get into it. I'd invited him, but once again, he'd had an excuse. A while ago, Cal had told me small groups weren't his thing, but these people were a huge support system for me, and it was hard not to take it personally that he didn't want to get to know my friends. Still, I told myself to respect his decision and give him time to come around.

As we sat on the couch, concern filled Evan's handsome face, and I could tell he was about five seconds away from launching into high school guidance counselor mode.

Not gonna happen, dude. "Have you heard from Kelsey? I emailed her a few days ago but haven't heard back."

"She's getting settled," he said. "Dealing with culture shock, but she loves the adventure."

Kelsey and Evan had agreed to pray about continuing their relationship while she worked as a nurse in a clinic in Ethiopia. Would she ever come back, or would God ask her to stay overseas? "Have you ever felt called to serve as a missionary?" I stuffed the rest of the cookie in my mouth and wadded my napkin.

Evan scrubbed his hand over his stubbly chin. "The public school is my mission field."

There was no mistaking the pain that flashed in his hazel eyes, and my heart hurt for him. He truly loved Kelsey, which ruined Ashley's theory about me missing the boat with Evan.

"I heard a rumor that you've been looking into Zach's case since you were the one who found him," he said.

I wasn't the only one good at subject changing. "Where'd you hear that?"

He grinned. "The school secretary's a great source when she gets her coffee fix at Latte Conspiracies."

Oh, the joys of living in a small town. "It's true."

"What have you figured out?"

I told Evan about Zach's last word and the poisoned tea. "Do you know anything about a teenager dying from Jimsonweed poisoning this past summer?"

He shook his head. "This is the first I've heard of it."

"Well, it's a weird coincidence. I mean, anyone who wanted to grow the flowers could buy the seeds online—except in certain states—but I'd bet the average person doesn't know how poisonous they are. Unless they garden or are a plant expert."

"Yeah. It's like someone who knew the teens got the idea from them. Other kids, maybe?"

"Exactly." Had Zach ticked off one of the teens he worked with enough that they'd killed him? "Except..." I hadn't planned to bring up the break-in.

"What?"

"I think this situation is bigger than a teenager with a beef against a youth minister." I told him about the SUV following me and the break-in, and when the horror grew in his expression, I wondered if Ashley was right after all.

No. Not going there. He cares about me as a friend and maybe not even that. It wasn't like he'd checked on me after hearing that I'd found Zach.

"The people who broke in were looking for something in particular." I studied Brandi's Christmas tree. Every year she rotated themes, and this year she'd used her basketball, soccer, baseball, football, golf, and tennis ornaments.

"Something they thought was on your computer."

I gaped at him as a strange look settled over his expression.

"Yeah." I leaned forward. "Do you know something? Because if you do—"

"Nope." He shoved half a Santa cookie in his mouth, wadded up his napkin, and shot off the couch.

Yeah. Right. Evan had always been a terrible liar, and he obviously hadn't improved. I shrugged as I headed back to the kitchen for another cookie. I'd figure it out eventually.

I arrived at WSCC early Monday morning armed with the newest beverage from Latte Conspiracies—the Loch Ness Latte. There were plenty of finishing touches to add to the set before the Christmas program this weekend, and Ruby had made it clear she expected my presence.

As soon as I entered the greenroom, Ruby waved. "Good morning. Go out on stage and ask Doug what he needs you to do."

"Okay." I found Doug standing on a lift in the auditorium, hanging stars from the ceiling.

"Good morning!" I yelled.

"Hey, Georgia." Doug looked down at me. "We could use some help painting the time machine." He motioned upstage to an old-fashioned sleigh. "The outside needs a coat of black, and the time-travel dashboard needs detail work."

I moved closer to examine it. Someone had fastened a wood panel with buttons and knobs in front of the bench. Perfect for navigating back in time.

Thank goodness I'd worn an old long-sleeved T-shirt leftover from my college days and a pair of jeans from the same era. I took a little bit of pride that I could still fit into them in spite of my thighs being bigger than I'd like.

I glanced around the stage and saw brushes, a drop cloth, and some rags. "Where's the paint?"

Doug slapped his palm to his forehead. "I knew I forgot something in the storage barn this morning." He pressed a button on the lift, and it came down with a buzz.

"I'll get it."

He lifted his finger off the button. "That'd be a big help. Ruby wants these stars done ASAP, and I have a lot more to go." He pointed to the glittery pile at his feet.

"Do we need any other colors?"

"Yep. Brown for the inn. Ebony for the sleigh, and there's a multi-colored set for all of those buttons and knobs on the dashboard—but you may want to let Ruby handle that part since it's her vision."

I chuckled. "Yeah, you don't want me anywhere near the detail work." The last time I'd had to take art had been in middle school, and the only thing that had saved me from getting a C—and missing the honor roll—was my ability to memorize facts about artists and regurgitate that information on tests.

Doug unhooked a key ring from the carabiner on his belt

loop, knelt down, and dropped them into my outstretched hand. "The barn key has a seven on it. Paint's on the shelf in the back."

I retrieved my coat from a chair, exited the church, and hoofed it across the parking lot to the large pole barn on the edge of the property. I was halfway there when my phone rang. I rolled my eyes when I saw who was calling.

"What's going on, Austin?" I stepped onto the gravel path.

"I'm fine. Except that you haven't needed my sidekick services, and that's been killing me."

I rolled my eyes as I approached the side door. "Sorry."

He heaved a sigh. "You could at least try to sound sincere after everything Presty and I did for you."

His tone reminded me of a mother doling out a first-class guilt trip to her wayward child. "Anyway, Preston and I bought a bike for Jill and Dad. We found a top-of-the-line model on sale down in Indy."

"Great." I slipped the key into the lock. "How much do I owe you?"

"Don't you want to see it first?"

"I'm sure whatever you've bought is perfect." Especially if it was top-of-the-line. I opened the barn door, and a mixture of gasoline fumes and mildew filtered out.

"I've got a couple looking at a house in Wildcat Springs this afternoon, so I'll stop by your farm for show and tell."

I patted the wall until I found the light switch. "If you come then, the only one you'll be showing the bike to is Gus. I'm at my church getting ready for our Christmas program this weekend."

"You're in a program, and you didn't invite me? Sissy, you break my heart." He let out an exaggerated moan.

"I can tell." I dodged two lawn mowers and found the shelves that contained at least twenty cans of paint in varying colors. Someone had labeled the lids with the room in the church where the paint had been used. "You'll probably never recover." I spotted the plastic-wrapped package of red, yellow, blue, green, and orange paints and set it on the concrete floor.

"Never make light of man's ability to die from a broken heart."

That should be Life Lesson #105. I choked back a laugh as I set the brown paint next to the multicolored package. *No sense in encouraging him.* "If you and Preston want to come, Mom and Dan will be here Friday night. At seven."

Nice Georgia.

The invitation was a small win in the kindness department, but it was too early to pat myself on the back for successfully navigating this conversation.

"Will your boyfriend be there?"

He's not my boyfriend—yet. "On Saturday night." I pushed a can of Blushing Beauty, used in the ladies' room, aside. Where *was* the ebony paint?

"You made up with him?" He performed an encore of his kissing noises from the other night.

"Yep." I scooted aside a can of Lullaby, a pale blue-green shade used in the nursery. "Do you want to come or not?" My resolve to be nice had vanished, and I walked away from the paint shelf, so I could focus on extricating myself from this chat without hanging up on him.

"I hate being an afterthought."

"It never crossed my mind you'd be interested." At least he'd moved on from Cal.

Austin chuckled. "I'm not. I have a date Friday night—and Saturday."

"Same girl?" That question slipped out before I could stop myself—which was one of my biggest problems.

"No way. I'm not ready to settle down. Unlike you, I'm still young."

Jesus, help me. I jerked the phone away from my ear, and my finger hovered over the red button, itching to hang up. Instead, I put the phone back. "How. Much. Do I owe you?"

"I'll tell you when I swing by the church this afternoon. Catch you later, sissy."

I scowled and shoved my phone into my pocket. Dan or his first wife *had* to have dropped Austin and Preston on their heads.

Turning my attention back to the paint shelf, I shoved away cans of River Stone, picked up a smaller can, and examined the writing on the lid. *Electric Tangerine—Zach's office.*

A wave of sadness rolled over me.

Zach must've liked vivid colors since he'd been wearing a bright blue jacket the day he died. I swallowed over the lump in my throat and put the can on the shelf, but an extra clatter caused me to stop. I picked it up and shook. This time there was no mistaking the rattle, so I pried off the lid.

A flash drive rested in the can.

CHAPTER THIRTEEN

I bit my lip as I examined the flash drive. The letters *ZJM* had been scrawled in permanent marker on the side.

Zach's initials? I pulled out my phone and typed *Zachary Mishler obituary* into the search engine.

A second later I had confirmation. His middle name was James.

Why would he have put a flash drive in a paint can? Did Doug know anything about it? He was the only one who accessed the barn on a regular basis. Had he hidden it?

I needed to give it to Cal as soon as possible, in case it was evidence, but I wanted to look at what was on it first. Judging from the amount of work left to do on the set, I'd be trapped at church all day, and it'd probably be at least nine o'clock before I made it home after choir practice.

Even if I invented an excuse about needing to use Mona's computer, it didn't seem like a bright idea to use one of the church's to snoop. I'd just say I was going home to let Gus out at lunchtime—which wouldn't be a lie. Though I hadn't had time to replace the computer that'd been stolen, I had my old college laptop stashed away in a closet. Hopefully, it'd still work.

I finally located the ebony paint and locked the storage shed. On my way back inside, I stopped at my truck, stowed Zach's can under a blanket in the back seat, and returned to the church to paint the time machine.

"Sissy!" A couple of hours later, Austin stood at the back of the church auditorium with his hands lifted in the air as if he were praising Jesus.

The other people working—Ruby, Doug, Mona, and Carsyn—turned and stared at my stepbrother.

I put down the brush that I'd been using to paint the door of the inn, and conviction washed over me at the thought of Jesus and Austin. My stepbrothers annoyed me so much that I'd never given a thought about where they stood spiritually.

I needed to keep that thought in mind as I interacted with Austin and Preston—starting immediately. I wiped my hands on a rag and stood. "How'd your showing go?"

He put his hand on his heart. "Awww. You care." He shook his head. "This old married couple has been looking at houses for five years and can't agree. Their last agent retired before they could decide, so they got passed on to me."

"Lucky you."

He shrugged. "Makes life interesting. They didn't dig this house either. Big surprise."

We went outside to Austin's black SUV, which was parked next to my truck. He opened the hatch and motioned toward the bike. "What do you think?"

"Mom will love the aqua color. It's pretty."

"That's what Preston said. It has all the fancy stuff for Dad, but Jill would care most about the color. Presty somehow remembered her favorite is blue."

As if that could've been hard. Mom had used it all over their house when they'd redecorated. "What do I owe you?"

"One hundred twenty-five." He took the receipt from his pocket and gave it to me. For a second, I was proud of him for producing it without a battle.

I did the math in my head. "Looks good. I'll send the money to you by the end of the week." I returned the receipt.

"I'd be thrilled to take your money since I have dates this weekend, but Preston put it on his card. That goody-goody insisted I bring the receipt and show you." He smirked.

I should've known I'd given Austin too much credit.

I was about to say good-bye and make a getaway when a commotion next to the church caught my attention. Cal, Detective Kimball, and a couple of deputies from the sheriff's department were entering the building.

"Whoa," Austin said. "They mean business. You in trouble?"

I knit my brows. "No." Now that Cal was here, any excuse to hold onto the flash drive had been obliterated. I had to act fast before I did my duty and handed it over. I stepped behind Austin's SUV. "Do you have your laptop with you?"

"Yeah. Why?"

I cringed inwardly. "I need you to be my sidekick. Again."

His eyes lit up. "Don't be messing with me." He pressed his hand to his heart. "I couldn't take it."

"I'm serious." I punched the keypad on my truck and unlocked it. Throwing the blanket aside, I retrieved the paint can.

"You hid paint under a blanket? That's weird—even for you, sissy."

I rolled my eyes. "Someone hid a flash drive in here." I shook the can. "I want to see what's on it before I turn it over to Cal. I found it this morning when I was searching for paint, and it might have something to do with Zach's murder because it has his initials on it."

I expected a snide comment about me painting, but Austin opened the door on the driver's side before turning to me. "What are you waiting for? Get in!"

I jogged around the vehicle and shut myself inside. It smelled like a mix of stale French fries and Austin's cologne. Otherwise, it was spotless, as if he'd had it detailed.

He reached into the back seat and took his laptop out of the case. "It better not put a virus on my computer."

"Don't you want to see what's on it?"

"Duh. I just don't want to destroy my computer."

I pulled a glove out of my coat pocket and put it on before I took out the drive and shoved it into his computer. A list of two JPEG files and a movie file showed on the menu.

Austin opened the first file—a real estate listing for a two-story colonial in Richardville.

"Boy. We've stumbled onto a real terrorist plot here." Austin chuckled. "Maybe Zach was looking for a house and was comparing prices." He pointed at the date on the screen. "This place sold a month ago, and somebody got a good deal." He slid his finger down to the purchase price compared to the website's estimate of the property value. "Way below market value."

"What's the other picture?" I asked.

The photo showed four tiny houses on wheels grouped around a pond.

Weird. "I've never seen a tiny house camp around here."

"Me neither," he said.

I pointed to the screen. "Let's watch the video."

Austin clicked *play*, and a room painted seafoam green came into focus. Hanging on the wall was a large white anchor with a distressed finish. The camera panned left to right, revealing a circle of empty chairs.

"What *is* this?" Austin asked.

"The wall decoration makes me wonder if it's a meeting at the Anchor Recovery Center in Richardville. They have group meetings for people with gambling addictions."

"Aren't those meetings supposed to be anonymous?"

I looked at him. "You're right. Why would they allow a camera?"

"Because they didn't know. The person filming was probably wearing a hidden camera. I may or may not have a friend who has a hat camera."

I didn't even want to think about what he and Preston had used that for, but I tucked that fact away. It might come in handy someday.

I focused on the video. Had Doug filmed a group therapy session? If so, why? "Is the sound on?"

He checked. "All the way. A lot of those cameras don't record audio."

I snorted. "Is that what your friend told you?"

His eyes gleamed. "Yep."

A young couple holding hands entered and sat. A woman wearing a chunky beaded necklace entered, and a guy with dark-framed glasses and a prominent nose followed. They all greeted each other, and from what I could tell, there was small talk. At last, a man with a bushy beard entered, and I took a good look at his face.

It was Tristan Phillips—Jim's brother who volunteered at Solid Rock Mission. Was he a group leader at Anchor Recovery Center? The group stood and joined hands. Tristan spoke, and they appeared to be repeating what he said.

"I wish I could read lips," Austin said.

"Me too."

When Tristan finished, they let go of each other's hands, and he went around the circle, greeting each person. Tristan made it to the person filming, and I watched his mouth carefully, hoping he'd say the person's name, but it looked like he said, "Welcome."

The video cut to a new scene—a small office with a bright red laptop sitting on a desk. Sitting next to the laptop was a certificate. The person filming moved closer, but I felt like I was on a theme park ride when the camera whipped around.

A scowling Tristan stood in the doorway. He pointed out the door, and the camera moved up and down. The view changed to the hallway.

"That person is totally wearing a hat camera," Austin said.

The recording ended, and Austin and I groaned—in unison—which was completely disturbing.

"Back it up and see if you can catch the name on the certificate."

He went back to the desk view and zoomed in. "It's pretty blurry, and I can't see what the rest of the certificate says, but I think the name is Jody Chatfield."

"Yeah, I agree." I gnawed my lip. "Obviously someone was snooping in Tristan's office. But why? And is Jody Chatfield important?"

"Good questions. Since I'm your devoted sidekick, I'll give them some thought, but I've got to get back to the office. Let me copy these files real quick."

When he finished, I put the drive back in the paint can. "Thanks for your help." I hopped out of the SUV.

"Any time, sissy." He cranked the engine.

I waved as he screeched out of the parking lot. As soon as I entered the church, I walked into chaos.

Ruby rushed up to me. "Your boyfriend's here with a search warrant. Oh, it's simply terrible timing. What'll we do if they're still here when it's time for rehearsal?"

"Practice while they're searching."

"Oh, it will be a dreadful distraction." She rested her hand on her forehead. "We'll never be ready. The show will be a disaster. A *disaster*, I tell you."

I guided Ruby toward her office in the greenroom. "How about some water?"

"Please." She pointed to her desk drawer. "Get me some Teddy Grahams too. My sugar's dropping."

Thankfully, she was too distracted to interrogate me about the paint can I was toting, but not wanting to press my luck, I produced her snack quickly and went to look for Cal. I found him in the library, along with Detective Kimball and two deputies who were conducting a search of the books.

"What's going on? I step out to see the bike my stepbrother bought our parents, and I come back to...this."

Cal set his jaw. "We have a search warrant. We received a tip this morning."

"Are you looking for something in particular?"

"A flash drive that may've been hidden in a book safe."

"Here." I opened the paint can and held it, so he could see inside. "I found this on the shelf in the storage barn this morning. It rattled when I put it away. I was going to turn it in to you as soon as I had a chance because it had Zach's initials on it, but we've been busy and—"

"Have you looked at it?" His tone held a note of sternness as he took the can.

Detective Kimball gazed at me. I opened my mouth to answer truthfully, but Cal held up his hand.

"Never mind. I don't want to know."

"Probably just as well," I said. "Who gave you the tip?"

"I'm not going to say."

I'd find out anyway because after Evan's weird behavior the night before, I had a pretty good idea where to start looking. "Okay, then." I pointed to the door. "We've still got a lot of work to do on the set, so I'd better get back at it."

He glanced over his shoulder at the deputies and Detective Kimball who were focused on the search before dropping a quick kiss on my cheek. "I'll call you later," he whispered as he took a second peek at his coworkers.

With a spring in my step, I returned to the stage where I resumed painting the inn door. A few minutes later, Doug entered with an armful of boards. When he set them down, I motioned for him to come over. Was there a delicate way to ask about the video on the flash drive? If there was, the solution was escaping me.

"Lot of chaos around here," he said as he moved closer.

"No kidding." I looked around. "Did Zach ever say anything to you about hiding a flash drive in the storage barn?"

Genuine surprise flitted through Doug's expression. "Nope. That where they found it?"

"I found it. In an empty paint can."

Doug tilted his head. "Why would he hide it there?"

I shrugged. "Why would he feel the need to hide it at all?"

"You get a look at it?" He grinned as if he already knew the answer.

"It has a copy of a real estate listing, a picture of four tiny houses—and hidden camera footage of a man named Tristan Phillips leading some kind of meeting." I motioned for him to come closer. "Does Tristan lead group sessions at Anchor?" I whispered.

He squinted. "None that I've been to—and I don't recognize the name either."

"Do you know someone named Jody Chatfield?"

"Nope." He shoved his hands in his overall pockets. "I'm sorry."

I dumped the empty box from Pizza Heaven into the church's dumpster and rubbed my greasy hands on my paint-splattered jeans as I crossed the parking lot. The supreme pizza that'd tasted yummy going down had settled into a hard lump in my gut. Good thing I was directing instead of singing because that wouldn't have been pretty.

Truth be told, I was finding it hard to transition into director mode, when all I wanted to do was go home, relax, and try to make sense of everything I'd learned today.

I hadn't made it home for lunch or even later that afternoon to change. In fact, I'd placed a frantic call to Brandi and had asked her to feed and let poor Gus out.

Unless Doug was lying about knowing Tristan Phillips, he probably hadn't been the one who filmed at Anchor Recovery Center. What if Zach had attended the group session because he had a gambling problem too? But why wouldn't Doug have just told me that? Unless he was trying to protect Zach's reputation.

Then there were the houses. Pictures of the properties alone wouldn't be suspicious, but the fact that the flash drive had been hidden caused me to wonder about their significance. Plus, there might not even be a connection between the pictures and the video. With a sigh, I opened the door and entered the building.

Time for choir practice.

CHAPTER FOURTEEN

Tuesday morning, I got up early to put my farming hat back on. While Grandpa and I had been winterizing our equipment, we'd discovered one of our combines was in need of repairs beyond our expertise. After shuffling tractors and other equipment around to get the combine out of my pole barn, I drove it down the back roads to Wildcat Springs Implement so a mechanic could fix it.

I chatted with J.T. and the owner Max Jenkins awhile, and then Grandpa and Wanda arrived to pick me up and take me home. I hopped in the back seat of Grandpa's extended cab truck.

"We were thinking about having lunch at Velda's. Want to join us?" Grandpa asked.

"Absolutely." As usual, lunch options at my house were scarce.

"I've been meaning to ask." Grandpa glanced in the rearview mirror. "You started prepping for taxes yet?" Grandpa had handed all of the bookkeeping tasks over to me when I'd started farming with him.

"No, sir. I've barely had time to put the files in order after the break-in."

He didn't comment, which was worse than if he'd expressed disapproval.

"Now, Ron, she's been busy with the church program. She's got plenty of time to get to it," Wanda said. "How's the program going, dear?" She wore her silver hair in a short, asymmetrical cut, which gave her a youthful and energetic appearance.

I twisted Grandma Winston's amethyst ring that I'd inherited after her death four years ago. She'd always jumped to my defense, and Wanda had begun to fill that role, which meant she was perfect for Grandpa.

"The choir's ready. I'm going tonight to watch the drama portion. We'll put everything together on Wednesday and Thursday."

"We're looking forward to it," Wanda said. "My son and daughter-in-law are coming with us Friday night."

"I'd like to meet them."

Wanda beamed. "They're looking forward to meeting you."

A few minutes later, we rolled into downtown Wildcat Springs, and Grandpa parked in the public lot across the street from Velda's. A brisk wind hit us as we crossed the street and took refuge in the crowded restaurant. The café's soft yellow walls displayed historic pictures of Wildcat Springs. Mismatched tables and chairs added to the vintage charm.

Wanda snagged a table while Grandpa and I waited in line to order.

The line moved forward, and I decided the chicken pot pie—on special—would hit the spot on this chilly day.

"I bought a ring," Grandpa muttered, and for a second, I wondered if I'd heard him correctly, but when I looked at him, his expectant expression pushed that doubt away.

"Cool. For Christmas?" I whispered. Why Grandpa had

chosen to drop this information in the middle of Gossipville was beyond me, but I didn't want him to think I was displeased with his news.

"Yes."

"Have you told Aunt Rhonda?" My dad's sister was a dental hygienist and lived with her husband in Indianapolis.

He nodded. "She's thrilled." He leaned closer. "I even asked Wanda's son for permission."

"He gave it, right?"

"Sure did." Grandpa lifted his chin.

"Do you need help planning the proposal?" I whispered.

"What now?" He gaped at me and then chuckled. "No. There's no need for something fancy, especially at our age. All those elaborate proposals make me wonder if you young gals want the relationship or just some romantic experience and a big wedding.

It wasn't lost on me that he'd said *you young gals*. Was that why I was having so much trouble picking a gift for Cal? I'd set expectations for myself that were too high—or I'd even been expecting too much of him.

I just needed to relax and quit trying so hard.

After Grandpa and Wanda dropped me off at home, I got in my truck with a sweet tea from Velda's. I drove to Wildcat Springs Junior-Senior High School where I checked in with Mrs. Sanders. She'd been the secretary when I'd gone to school there, so after telling me about her three grandbabies, she sent me to Evan's office.

I knocked on his doorframe. "Hey. Mrs. Sanders told me to come on back."

"Have a seat." He didn't glance up from his computer screen, and his fingers flew across the keyboard. "Be with you in a second."

Sitting in front of his desk reminded me of the one time I'd been sent to the principal's office in junior high. I'd had to go the restroom during lunch, and my bladder didn't feel like waiting on the sour-faced supervisor to waddle over to our table to grant us permission to get up. She'd chased me into the girls' room, hauled me out of the stall, and dragged me to the office.

Mr. Carlyle had laughed and sent me back to class via the restroom.

"Sorry." Evan looked up. "Just had to finish sending that email. What brings you by?"

I held out the tea. "I wanted to brighten a friend's day."

"Right." He laughed. No—he *guffawed*.

I needed to do more random acts of kindness. Then it wouldn't be so transparent when I wanted information.

"Sorry." He pressed his lips together, but his eyes were still filled with amusement. He took the tea. "Thanks. That's nice of you."

"Since you see through me, I'll get right to it. Did you call in a tip to the sheriff's department about a flash drive hidden in a book safe?" I crossed my legs and set my handbag on the floor.

"Sure did. I take it the police showed up at the church with a search warrant?"

"Yep. Yesterday afternoon. Why didn't you tell me about it?"

"What would you have done if I *had* told you?"

"I would've suggested you call Cal and—"

"Really, Georgia? You wouldn't have gone to the church that very night and looked through all the books in the building until you found the flash drive?"

I bounced my leg. "You're right. I would've." After all, I did have a key, thanks to Ruby.

"I know. I was trying to keep you safe."

I met his gaze, not wanting to unpack the meaning behind his actions. Just brotherly concern, right? "Will you at least tell me how you knew about the flash drive?"

"Did they find it?"

"I did. By accident." I filled him in on how I'd made the discovery, but I didn't tell him about looking at the contents.

"Mysteries seem to find you." He shook his head. "About a month ago, I stopped by the church to pick up brochures about the mentoring program that Zach was coordinating. We've had some kids dealing with heavy stuff this year—drug overdoses, underage drinking, depression, pregnancy. You name it. We were hoping this program might help. Anyway. Mona told me to go back to Zach's office. His door was open, but he didn't hear me. He was putting a flash drive into a hollowed-out book."

"Did he ever realize you saw him?"

"Nope. I figured the guy had a right to privacy, so I backed out and let a few seconds pass before I knocked on the doorframe. I didn't even think of it until you started talking about your computer being stolen."

"Thanks for telling me." I stood. "I won't keep you."

"Hold on. There's one more thing you might like to know."

I sat. "Go on."

"Today at lunch I asked about the kid who died from Jimson-weed poisoning last summer, and one of the teachers knew. The victim was from Indianapolis, but his girlfriend is from Richardville. Apparently she tried the Jimsonweed too, but the tiny dose didn't kill her—just messed her up for a while."

"Did you get names?"

"The boy was Eli Mossburg, and the girl is Mia Phillips."

It took me a second to remember where I'd heard the girl's name. Then it hit me. Jim's daughter. Which meant Mona had lied about getting the information about Jimsonweed at her cycling class.

Had she done it to protect Mia's privacy, or did she have a darker reason for hiding the truth?

When I arrived home from my visit with Evan, I finally got around to hanging Ashley's mistletoe in the opening between my foyer and my living room. Then, I entertained Gus for a bit before dragging myself into my office.

I stalled by searching for Jody Chatfield on social media and found a few people by that name—men and women—but no one in the area.

Finally, I made myself finish organizing my files so I could begin tax prep for our farm. Gus lay by the door and napped, which was what I would've preferred to do.

Though I tried to focus, my mind kept wandering to Cal. I needed to relax about the whole Christmas gift thing. The idea would come. Beverly's advice about figuring out how to love him reverberated in my head. What made him feel special?

I stretched for a minute before opening my email. Kelsey had finally responded.

Hey Georgia,

Sorry I haven't had a chance to get back with you, but it's been crazy here. First, you should know that Cal's a private person, so if he's not super open with you at first, don't take it personally. It's just his way. Plus, I don't want to say too much, but his family is going through a difficult time, so that's probably weighing on him.

I'll definitely be praying that you'll figure out what to get Cal. (I wasn't sure what to get Evan, when I came across this totally cool wall hanging. It's the continent of Africa with a heart over Ethiopia. Perfect, right?)

I took a timeout to throw up a little in my mouth.

Cal is totally hard to buy for, so don't feel like it means anything significant about your relationship. One year, our grandma threatened to knit him a sweater with Yoda on the front if he didn't tell her what he wanted.

He got a Yoda sweater. Have him show you sometime. You'll think of something perfect because you're awesome like that.

Praying for you!
    Love,
    Kelsey

I rested my elbows on my desk, buried my head in my hands, and groaned. Gus walked over to make sure I wasn't dying, and I patted his head.

I'd just refocused on taxes when my doorbell rang. Gus charged out of my office, and I trudged behind him and peered through the sidelight.

Austin.

Well, I was ninety percent sure it was Austin and not Preston, because he'd made a comeback as my sidekick. Since a chance remained it was Preston, I settled for a simple *hey there* when I opened the door.

"You *still* can't tell us apart?" He leaned against the door.

I stepped aside and motioned for him to come in. "Sure I can. Austin's the snarky one. Preston's the nice one."

Austin snorted. "Whatever. Here's a pro tip." He pointed

underneath his left eye. "I've got a scar from falling on the corner of the fireplace when I was three."

"Thanks." My cheeks warmed. How had I never noticed that before? "What's going on?"

"I figured now that we're working together, I should help you out." He patted Gus's head, but when the dog's nose slimed his navy dress pants, he stepped back.

"Sorry," I said.

He shrugged. "It'll wash off. I had another showing over here, so I thought I'd swing by and tell you what I found out."

"About what?" I tried to remember how we'd left our last conversation.

"Seriously? How did you ever solve a murder?" He shook his head and puffed out his chest. "Digging deeper is key."

Slime his pants again, Gus. Oh, how I longed for the power of telepathy. Instead, God reminded me to love my stepbrother.

"You're right." I nearly choked on the words and motioned him into the dining room. I pointed at the board and picked up a piece of blue chalk. "What can you add?"

"That's an impressive murder board, sissy." He sat facing the wall. "I asked around about the four tiny houses. One of my colleagues told me there's a ten-acre property about ten miles east of here. Some people who are into that living simply thing are putting their tiny houses there because of the pond and a big woods. But that's not the interesting part."

"Okay." I wrote *tiny houses* and *ten-acre property* on the board.

"I searched records, and Final Rejuvenation, LLC owns the property—and the colonial house that sold for cheap." He grinned. "Want to guess who sold the house to Final Rejuvenation?"

"Jody Chatfield?"

"Ding, ding, ding!"

I let Austin's words sink in. "Do you know who owns Final Rejuvenation?" I scrawled the company name on the board.

"Not yet, but it shouldn't be hard to figure out."

I had to give him major credit since he'd been way more helpful than I could've ever imagined. I reached across the table for a high five. "Nice work."

He smacked my palm. "There's more."

"Really?"

"Yep. I was having lunch with my buddy Ryan who works at Heartland Real Estate, and I was telling him how I was helping you with Zach Mishler's murder investigation." He cocked his head while a few seconds ticked by.

Merciful heavens. "Spit it out." I tried hard to keep the edge out of my tone, but my effort failed. Big time.

"Patience," he crooned and held up a hand in the manner of a guru.

Sic him, Gus. No, no. Nice Georgia. Jesus loves Austin, and so should I. "My apologies." I pressed my hands together and bowed.

He smirked. "Ryan said Zach was getting his real estate license. He'd completed the course and was scheduled to take the exam. Heartland Real Estate had hired him to start at the beginning of the year."

"Wow." I added that information to the board. "Doug told me Zach had resigned, but I had no idea he was leaving ministry completely."

It was interesting that Zach had planned to stay in Indiana instead of going back to Michigan to work for his dad. Had Olivia motivated him to stay? Plus, if he was ready for the exam, he had to have been working on the class for a while—long before the argument with Pastor Mark.

Austin shrugged. "You know how church people can be. He'd

probably had enough." He flicked his gaze away and made me wonder about his own history.

Why had I never given that more thought? "Christians aren't perfect."

"No kidding." He scowled as he stood up and pushed in his chair. "Anyway, Farthing out." He saluted and walked to the door.

"Thanks for the info." I swallowed. "You're a good sidekick."

"I know." He winked. "Later, sissy." He waved as he bolted down the sidewalk.

***

"Cut!" Ruby barked.

That night, the orchestra groaned to a stop, but a single flute trilled for a few seconds longer than the rest as the cast grew silent.

"No, no, *no!*" Ruby waved her arms, and with jowls shaking, thundered down the church aisle toward Rob, who sported a look of utter confusion on his handsome face as he swayed above the stage in a harness attached to two wires.

Rob adjusted his left angel wing and batted aside a star that I'd already noted needed to be moved. "What'd I do wrong now?"

"It's *ye shall find.* Not *you will find.* Get it right." Ruby stomped her foot. "This is the birth announcement of our Lord and Savior!"

My head throbbed, and I'd been feeling fine before rehearsal that night. How had Jessica Myers put up with this? I set aside the notepad Ruby had thrust in my hands at the beginning of practice, got up, and walked toward our over-wrought director. Diplomacy was going to be a challenge when I wanted to run from the room screaming—but thankfully—not cussing.

God and I must be making progress where my mouth was concerned.

I stopped at center stage where children dressed as sheep gazed up at Rob, while their dads, garbed as shepherds, leaned on their wooden crooks. On stage right, Leah sat in the time machine sleigh with Millie the Time-Traveling Scientist.

"Um, Ruby," I said, "modern Bible translations use the words *you will*."

When Ruby had complained about Rob's inability to learn his lines, she'd failed to mention her insistence that they come from the King James Version. Her doggedness was even weirder considering that Pastor Mark *never* used that translation in his sermons.

"But King James English is simply wonderful. It fits my vision for this program."

"The music is modern."

"It sounds more angelic to say *shall* and *ye*."

I locked eyes with Rob, who shook his head. If I'd had to guess, I'd have put him about ten seconds from unhooking himself and splatting on the stage below to experience sweet relief.

"You're doing great, Rob." I gave a thumbs up and faced Ruby. "He looks so angelic, I doubt the audience will notice his verb and pronoun choices."

On cue, Rob raised his arms.

Ruby heaved a sigh. "No one *ever* understands my vision."

Probably not, but I had to say something, while fighting the urge to begin my forthcoming words with *behold*.

Not the time, Georgia Rae.

I patted Ruby's shoulder. "Your vision is spectacular. You've done an amazing job. The set is gorgeous. The costumes are beautiful, and the cast is marvelous." I stopped before I ran out of adjectives.

"You think?"

"I know." The silence thickened as I looked around at cast and orchestra members who were avoiding eye contact.

A little help would be good, people.

"Let's hear it for Ruby." Rob the Mind Reader wolf-whistled.

A couple of sheep-children stood and clapped.

Ruby burst into tears. "Oh, thank you. You'll never know how much your support means." She sniffed and took a bow. "Let's start from the top of the scene, and Rob? I'll sacrifice my desires for the greater good." She clapped twice. "Carry on as you've memorized."

And it came to pass, that rehearsal continued without further incident.

CHAPTER FIFTEEN

"I can't believe you'd betray me like that."

I nearly lost my hold on my Moon Landing Mocha as I whirled around to face Austin on Wednesday morning at Latte Conspiracies. "What'd I do?"

I tried to process our last conversation. I'd thanked him for the information yesterday. He'd been too pleased with himself. Totally and completely normal.

He scowled. "Austin told me he's been your sidekick again. Bragged about it. After I was nice to you, you picked him over me?" He huffed and crossed his arms.

Preston. I was dealing with Preston. In my fuzzy-brained condition, I'd failed to notice the lack of a scar next to his eye. I longed for a sip of coffee, but Bobbi Sue had just made my drink, and I didn't need to add scalded taste buds to my growing list of troubles.

"I'm sorry, Preston." I motioned to an empty table. "Let's have a seat and talk. I'll explain everything."

A slow grin spread over his face, and a chuckle bubbled in his throat. He clapped his hands. "You should've seen the expression on your face. Why wasn't I ready with my camera?" He shook his head. "Total fail. Austy would've loved to see how panicked you looked."

I gritted my teeth. How much damage would hot coffee do to a pretty-boy face? He was about to find out.

"I had no idea you liked us that much," he said.

"Don't be so sure." I tightened my grip on my coffee cup.

He slapped my shoulder. "Aw. Lighten up, babe. I'm kidding. Sort of."

Nice Georgia. Jesus loves Preston too. I drew a deep breath. "Let's sit. Can I buy you a coffee?"

"No, I'm good."

"You came in here to stalk me."

"Totally." He pulled out a stool and sat.

"You know that's creepy, right?"

"Whatever. We're family." Preston folded his hands and rested them on the table. "Seriously, do you have something I can do? Some way I can help?" He sounded like an eager student waiting for an assignment from a teacher.

Life Lesson #501: Never underestimate the power of sibling rivalry.

I choked back a laugh. It was quite the dilemma. Should I give him a task to keep him busy and risk the consequences of encouraging him in this ridiculous sidekick business?

Since I was busy with the Christmas program, I decided to live dangerously. "You know, I've been wondering if Final Rejuvenation LLC owns other properties. Besides, Austin hasn't figured out who the owner is yet, so you—"

"I'm on it." He jumped up. "I'll call when I've got your answers." He darted out the door before I could say another word.

Sweet baby lambs in a pasture.

I ventured a sip of mocha and surveyed the room, expecting

to see patrons gawking at me after the ridiculous spectacle. Instead, Bobbi Sue was busy cleaning behind the counter. A couple of men worked at laptops, and two women were laughing at a table in the corner.

My eyes fell on a sign near the entrance to Miller's Books—the adjoining store that Bobbi Sue's husband Hemingway ran. According to the ad, they were having a pre-Christmas, forty-percent-off sale.

I should take a look and see if I could find a gift for Ashley. I'd already found an antique serving platter for Brandi at an estate sale in August. We never spent a lot of money on gifts for each other, but we always got each other a little something and made a night of exchanging presents.

I wandered into the bookstore where I found the Christian suspense section. As I surveyed the titles, I chewed my lip. Though I wasn't a reader, the books looked good. I just didn't know what Ashley had already read.

Dumb idea.

As I moved to the door, I caught sight of Cal. In the self-help section. Looking at relationship books. He held a book and flipped through the pages.

If I could get close enough to see what it was...

He slapped the book closed, stuck it back on the shelf, and started to turn.

I shot out of sight behind a shelf of romance books—the bodice-ripping kind. Mocha splashed onto my coat.

Biting back a naughty word, I dug in my purse for a tissue. Mopping my coat, I glanced around the shelf to see if he was still there.

"Good morning."

Heat crept into my cheeks as I faced Cal. "Morning. Beautiful day. You have to appreciate sunshine this time of year since we don't get very much of it in December. I came in to look for a

Christmas gift for Ashley, but I realized I don't know what books she's read, so that won't work very well, and since I don't read books that often, this was probably a bad idea."

He pointed to the shelf behind me. "She's into romance, I see."

"No. Uh. She likes Christian suspense. Clean stuff. Which is totally what I would pick. If I read books for fun." I tucked a stray hair behind my ears. "Do you like reading?" My voice had reached an unnaturally high pitch.

"As a matter of fact, I do, and I have quite the book collection." His blue eyes twinkled. "They're still boxed up in my spare room."

"What genre do you—?"

His phone jangled, and he held up a finger. "Perkins." His pleasant expression melted away, and his eyes darkened. "Where?" He shifted. "Be there in five."

He disconnected. "Sorry. Got to go." He leaned over and kissed my cheek.

"What happened?"

"Vic Sloan was fishing and found Olivia Scott's car submerged in his pond."

CHAPTER SIXTEEN

That afternoon, when I arrived at church to prepare for dress rehearsal, Mona greeted me with a sad smile.

"I'm glad you're here." She stood up from her desk. "You're good at calming Ruby down. I haven't had any luck, and Pastor Mark's gone."

Great. Now I had a reputation as the Ruby Whisperer. "What's wrong?" I leaned against the counter and wondered what the newest production catastrophe was.

"Carsyn called a few minutes ago and told her Vic Sloan found Olivia's car in his pond."

I nodded slowly. "Yeah. I heard. I'm praying it's *only* her car, so there's a chance she's still alive."

Vic's property was located between Wildcat Springs and Richardville, and it spanned a couple of acres. The east edge of the pond—a former rock quarry—wasn't that far from the highway.

"I hope so." Tears shone in Mona's eyes. "She's such a sweet girl, and she was planning to start selling makeup for me." She dabbed her eyes with a tissue. "I hate to think of her dying that way."

"Yeah." A lump welled in my throat. "That'd be awful."

She nodded. "Pastor Mark went to be with her dad."

Mona's reaction seemed sincere enough—unless guilt was the reason for her tears. I blew out a breath. "I'll go find Ruby." I motioned toward the greenroom.

As I approached the door, I tiptoed, expecting to hear sobbing. Instead, Ruby sat on the couch staring at the wall. Her gaze didn't move as I entered.

"Ruby?" I said softly.

"It could've been Carsyn." She blinked but didn't look at me.

I sat down next to Ruby. "Why?"

"Because I pushed her to date Zach. She could've been tangled up in this mess—like Olivia." Her tone was flat—almost robotic.

"You couldn't have known."

"I should've."

"Why?" Did Ruby have information about the killer?

"Mother's intuition."

I opened my mouth to protest but snapped it shut. I didn't know what to say—and Ruby shocking me into speechlessness was quite the accomplishment. Her nearly catatonic reaction seemed over-the-top, even for a drama queen. Still, a person didn't have to be close to someone to be affected by a tragedy. Sometimes it triggered buried feelings.

"How about some water?" That'd worked before.

"Please."

I walked over to her mini fridge. "This is the last one." I handed her the bottle.

Ruby cracked open the lid. "I don't mind sharing once in a while, but it's not my job to supply water—and Teddy Grahams —for the entire church. People have been helping themselves.

No one cares that I get low blood sugar," she said in a monotone.

Wait a second. Sharing.

Ruby's dwindling food and water stash jolted me into considering a different angle. Until now, I'd assumed that Zach had been the killer's primary target. Maybe even Olivia's target, which was why she'd vanished.

But what if Olivia truly was innocent, and the poisoned tea had been intended for her? Instead of drinking it herself, she'd shared it with Zach—because she knew he was a connoisseur. Then, what if the killer had tried another way to finish her off, and that's why her car was at the bottom of Sloan's Pond?

If that were the case, then we could be looking at a whole new group of suspects.

About twenty minutes before dress rehearsal started, Ruby came out of her daze and started bustling around as if she could work herself into forgetting the day's events. After scarfing down the honey-barbecue wings I'd ordered from Pizza Heaven, I changed into my biblical costume—minus the head covering—and was headed into the auditorium, when Pastor Mark passed me in the hallway and stopped.

"Just the person I wanted to see." He pointed to his office. "Do you have a minute?"

"Sure." Was I about to get a lecture because I'd disregarded his advice about staying out of the case?

He stepped aside so I could enter and motioned toward the chairs arranged in front of his desk. His Bible lay open next to his computer.

"What's on your mind?" I folded my hands and rested them in my lap.

"I owe you an apology." He took off his wool coat and hung it on a hook next to the door.

"For what?"

"The day you came to me and asked about Zach." He rolled out his plush, high-backed chair and sat. "I blew you off and discouraged you from investigating. Even brought your dad into it."

I'm used to it. "It's okay."

"No, it's not. I was dealing with my own guilt over coming down too hard on Zach for accidentally spending the night at Olivia's house." He emitted a wry chuckle. "Turns out she was helping him study for his real estate licensing exam, and they both fell asleep."

"I can see how that might happen." The edge of my mouth twitched. *Not the time, Georgia Rae.*

"I never should've laid a guilt trip on you for wanting to help —especially when God might be using you to help bring about justice."

I'd never thought of my meddling that way. "Thank you." I twisted the ends of the rope belt that gathered my tunic. "I need to ask you something else."

"Go ahead."

"Did Zach ever tell you why he was quitting youth ministry?"

Pastor Mark leaned forward. "He decided it wasn't the career for him. I offered to give him a good reference." He sighed. "I know there are rumors that I played a role in running him out so we could hire my son-in-law. The truth is, Zach wasn't here a month, and I sensed he already had one foot out the door. That irritated me, because no matter how much I tried to make him feel welcome, he wasn't fitting in."

"Why?"

"His heart wasn't in it. Ministry isn't easy, and he was getting pressure from his dad to quit and become a real estate agent. I think he hoped that if he made a career change, it would improve his relationship with his dad. My impression was that Zach never felt like he measured up to his older brother."

"That's sad." All of this information was interesting and cleared up any of my lingering doubts about Pastor Mark's innocence, but it wasn't getting me any closer to answers about Zach's death—and Olivia's disappearance. "Mona mentioned you were with Olivia's dad earlier. Was her body in the car?"

He shook his head. "No—and the divers didn't recover her from the pond either."

I rubbed my arms. Had she escaped her car just to be taken out by the killer in another way? "How's her dad?"

Sorrow flickered in his eyes. "A mess. She's his only child. He needs our prayers."

"Is Jon coming to the show?" I asked Brandi as I buttoned my coat that night after rehearsal.

She put on her leather gloves. "He'll be here Friday night." Her matter-of-fact tone didn't convey any excitement.

We hunched against the cold as we walked to our vehicles, which were parked side-by-side.

Beep, beep!

Rob stopped his car next to my truck and rolled down the window. "Evening ladies." He poked his head out. "Georgia, I wanted to thank you for standing up for me the other night at rehearsal."

"No problem. You're a great angel." I shoved an imaginary sock in my mouth. No need to disparage Ruby. "You did even better tonight."

"Thanks. Hey, would you like to have dinner sometime?"

Ducking her head, Brandi slipped away and got in her car.

The deluge of men I'd prayed for a couple of months ago continued to materialize. "Um...well...I'm seeing someone. But thank you." I glanced around the parking lot to see if anyone else had overheard, but Brandi was the only one. I didn't want it getting back to Cal that I'd been flirting with another guy. Although it might not hurt since Cal still hadn't told me he wanted to be exclusive.

Disappointment flickered in Rob's expression for a second before it rebounded into a toothy smile. "All right. Well, if it doesn't work out..."

"I appreciate the offer."

He nodded. "Could you do me a favor, though?"

"What?"

He shifted. "That Carsyn chick? Before you took over for Jessica, Carsyn was at a couple drama rehearsals helping her mom, and we talked. Now she keeps messaging me. I've tried to be nice, but she's not getting the hint that I'm not interested."

Nothing like a stalker chick to make a man's motives clear. Rob obviously had hoped that by taking me on a date, he'd discourage Carsyn. No surprise. That was how things usually went for me.

Until Cal.

I shoved my hands in my pocket. Carsyn must've broken up with the man that Ruby'd been worried about. "How can I help?'

"If she shows up to help her mom again and starts bugging me, will you find some director-y thing for me to do? Give me an assignment. Pull me aside to critique my performance. Anything."

"Sure. But have you thought about blocking her? That might help her get the hint."

"Totally." He lowered his voice. "But Carsyn's into some weird stuff, and I hate to cut her off in case she needs a friend."

"What kind of weird stuff?" I remembered what Ruby had

told me and how Mona had indicated that Carsyn was trying different religions.

He looked around the empty lot. "She's into a cult."

"What?" I flipped my scarf over my shoulder. "How do you know?" Goosebumps rose on my arms.

"She keeps talking about how her life's been adrift, and she's been searching. I asked her what she wanted that God couldn't provide, and she gave me some song and dance about Christianity being too restrictive."

She'd basically said the same thing during my manicure. "What'd she tell you about the cult?"

"They meet in that old country church between here and Richardville. Just bought it a couple of months ago. Anyway, she said her life is way more anchored now."

Anchored? I rested my hand on his car door as my breath hitched. "Did she tell you the name of the place?"

"Yeah. True Mooring Life Center."

CHAPTER SEVENTEEN

Taxes or finding out more about True Mooring Life Center? This was the dilemma I confronted the next morning while my coffee brewed. Considering the calendar had yet to roll over to the next year, there was no hurry.

True Mooring won the battle.

The night before, I'd nosed around online trying to learn more about the place, but I couldn't get anywhere because they didn't have a website—not even a Facebook page. I'd scoured Carsyn's Facebook and Instagram profiles hoping to find more information, but all she'd shared were inspirational memes, pictures of her cat, and photos of fancy nail designs she'd created.

I poured coffee into my Santa mug and ambled into my dining room where I wrote *True Mooring Life Center* on the board. Gus wandered over and perched next to me while I caffeinated and contemplated my next move.

After a full cup of coffee, I decided it was time to take Carsyn's suggestion and volunteer at Solid Rock Mission.

"You're totally my mom's hero," Carsyn said.

We were sitting on the floor in Jim Phillips's office at Solid Rock Mission stuffing envelopes with fundraising materials. When I'd called Carsyn to ask about volunteering, she'd told me she was planning to stop in before work, and I was welcome to join her.

"How so?"

"I heard about how you calmed Mom down the other night when Rob kept messing up his lines. Jessica Myers would've run out screaming—most people would've."

"Glad I could help." I added an envelope to a pile. "How's everybody at work doing with the news about Olivia's car?"

Carsyn's shoulders drooped, and she looked away. "Awful. Pretty much what you'd expect." She shivered and rubbed her arms. "Still, there's a possibility she's alive."

"I hope so. Hey, I know this is random, but do you know if Olivia was a tea drinker?" I kept my voice light—casual.

"Yeah. She and Zach were creating their own special blend for Christmas gifts." Her hand trembled as she put an envelope on the stack and met my gaze. "Anyway, if you need me to touch up your nails before the program, I'd be happy to." She glanced back and forth between my fingers and my eyes with a critical look that would've made her mother proud.

Nice Georgia. "I'll give you a call."

"Perfect. You'll want to look good for your boyfriend." She sounded as if she were trying to force cheerfulness into her tone. "How are things going with him?"

"Great." Except that he wasn't officially my boyfriend and hadn't even kissed me yet. *But other than that...* I folded a letter and stuffed it into an envelope. "Are you seeing anyone?"

"Yes." She giggled.

"Tell me about him."

"He's comp*let*ely amazing." She glanced down at her phone

and typed with her thumbs before putting it in her hoodie pocket. "He's *totally* helped me change my entire outlook on life."

"How so?" Apparently, the guy Ruby was worried about was still in the picture, and Rob had misread Carsyn's intentions.

"Have you ever wanted more out of life?" she whispered.

Begin sales pitch. Normally, that'd be an instance in which I'd actually run, but for the purpose of the investigation, I'd take the bait. "Don't we all?"

"What if there's a way to have it?" She rested her hands on top of a letter.

In spite of her peaceful-sounding words, something in her eyes unnerved me.

"Tell me more." I tried to sound casual as I straightened a tilting stack of letters.

"I've been searching for a while. I grew up going to church, but when I got older, it wasn't working for me." She shook her head. "But I don't dwell on it. I'd rather talk about how much True Mooring Life Center has helped me—and changed me."

Cue the inspirational music. "How?"

She slipped a letter in an envelope. "I've learned that I possess everything I need to be my own mooring. So do you—we all do."

Yeah, that was the total opposite of Christianity. "The guy you're dating helped you see this?"

"Yes." She beamed. "Tristan's *wonderful.*"

"Jim Phillips's brother Tristan—who volunteers here?"

"Yeah." She lowered her voice again. "He's like, twenty years older than me, but we connect, you know?"

Don't look grossed out. Don't look grossed out. "Sometimes that happens. Is Tristan in charge of True Mooring?"

"Yes. He's my mentor. We met when I started volunteering here."

The video. I'd assumed, because of the anchor on the wall,

that the group session with Tristan had taken place at Anchor Recovery Center. But it must have taken place at True Mooring Life Center instead. An anchor would fit with a mooring theme.

She straightened a stack of envelopes and put them in a box. "He's made *such* a difference in my life that I want to share it with everyone I meet." She rolled her eyes. "I scared Rob away, though. He totally thinks I have a thing for him, so I've been having a blast messing with his head." She picked a piece of lint off of her burgundy sweater. "But I shouldn't. As you can see, I'm still evolving. But it would be great if I could bring Rob into the fold."

In my head, I heard the theme music from *The Twilight Zone*. "Do you have meetings?"

"Tristan leads group sessions at the old church down the road, but he also meets with individuals."

"You meet in a church building, but you're not a church."

"Right. Tristan wanted to send the message that people can experience meaningful community and fellowship apart from organized religion. He's thumbing his nose at traditionalists by using that old building." She took the box of filled envelopes over to Jim's desk and then rejoined me.

"How does your family feel about Tristan?"

"You mean is my mom freaking out?" Carsyn shook her head. "Big time. She swears I'm in some kind of cult, but it isn't like that. We're a big family." She sighed. "To convince her I haven't gone off the deep end, I agreed to help with the Christmas program."

"So you're not completely opposed to Christianity."

"No. The faith has moral teachings that benefit society. Besides, I like Christmas. It's always been my favorite holiday." She picked up the silver anchor pendant on her necklace.

"That's pretty. Did Tristan give it to you?"

"I earned it after completing level two of the anchor system—the process we use to become our own mooring."

"How many levels?"

"Six—arise, negate, consecrate, harmonize, obey, rejuvenate—ANCHOR for short."

My heart thudded. *Anchor. Rejuvenate.* It couldn't be a coincidence that Final Rejuvenation LLC shared the name. "What do you have to do to get to the last level?"

"I'm not sure. You learn what's required as you advance to each level. Otherwise, it'd be too overwhelming."

That's probably an understatement.

She reached for her purse and removed a brochure. "Here you go. This will tell you about Arise, or level one. We'd love to have you join us at a session."

I forced a smile. "Thanks."

As soon as I left the mission, I got in my truck and skimmed through the brochure Carsyn had given me. The more I read, the more my stomach clenched. The focus of the brochure was Arise, but all six levels of ANCHOR were mentioned—though Carsyn was right in saying a person didn't find out much about them ahead of time. Arise was mostly about learning to let go of fear, anger, and negativity in order to become a better person.

Not bad things, of course. Even though I didn't agree with True Mooring's belief system, it didn't mean the group was doing anything criminal.

Still, my gut told me something was off with this group at the higher levels, and whoever had made that video had thought so too. I thought about the footage of the office and Jody Chatfield's name on the certificate. I considered the real estate listing and the picture of the tiny houses. What if Jody had sold her colonial and downsized to the tiny house compound to complete the ANCHOR system?

I sent a quick text to Austin.

Please send me the address of the property with the tiny houses.

I dropped my phone in my purse and sighed. This whole thing was creepy. Though Ruby expressed her concerns with fifty times more flair than most mothers, she had every reason to be freaking out.

Lord, please help Carsyn get out of this. Open her eyes to the truth.

Since I had plenty of time before our final dress rehearsal, I really wanted to visit True Mooring Life Center, but I had to call Cal and update him. I tapped his name on my phone and drummed the steering wheel.

"Hey, Georgia. What's going on?" His voice filled the cab.

"We need to meet—soon."

"I'm at the library in Wildcat Springs. Can you meet me in ten minutes or so?"

"I'm on my way."

Cal was waiting for me inside the library door. "I reserved a meeting room for us." He grasped my hand as we walked up the marble stairway to the second floor.

I surveyed him—handsome as usual in his khakis and blue-checked shirt—but something was missing. "Couldn't find a book?"

"They're in my car."

"What di—?"

"How's the Christmas program going?"

Okay, then. I can take a hint. I smothered a sigh. "Dress rehearsal had some hiccups last night, but we'll get them smoothed out tonight. If we don't, Ruby will have a meltdown."

He chuckled. "I'm sure you're a good influence." He opened the conference-room door.

"That's debatable." Walnut wainscoting lined the room, except for the wall with antique, floor-to-ceiling bookshelves.

"There's some nice craftsmanship in this room." He slid out a chair for me at the oval table in the middle of the room. "They don't make bookshelves like that anymore."

I sat, and he joined me. "Woodworking was one of my daddy's hobbies," I whispered. "He always loved the woodwork in this building."

He reached for my hand and squeezed it. "He had great taste."

"Yes." I pulled my hand away. "So...I volunteered at Solid Rock Mission with Carsyn Daniels this morning and got some interesting info." I told Cal what I'd learned from Carsyn about True Mooring and what Austin had shared about Jody Chatfield and Final Rejuvenation. "It can't be a coincidence that that last stage of the ANCHOR system shares a name with Final Rejuvenation, LLC. I'm wondering if people who graduate to the rejuvenate level have to sell their property to that company and then move into a tiny house."

"I see you managed to get a look at the flash drive." Cal steepled his fingers.

"Sorry." *But was I?*

"You sure about that?"

"I'm going to go with *no*."

"That's what I thought." His eyes twinkled as he leaned back. "But I can't be too upset since you uncovered a good lead. I'd never heard of True Mooring."

"Same here. I think it's a fairly new group. My theory is Carsyn invited Olivia to a session, and she sensed something shady was going on, so she went back to make a secret recording of a meeting and snoop around. When Tristan caught her, he was afraid she was going to expose some kind of secret, so he decided to kill her. He knew Jimsonweed is poisonous because his niece's boyfriend died after using it."

"I agree that Olivia was the killer's target," he said. "The morning he died, Zach sent her a text message thanking her for the tea."

I stared out the windows at Mohr Ice Cream and Candy across the street. "If Olivia didn't trust Tristan to the point where she made a secret recording, why would she accept tea from him —or pass it on to someone she cared about?"

"Tristan had to have an accomplice give her the tea—someone Olivia trusted."

"Like Carsyn Daniels," I said. "Except I'm having trouble seeing her willingly going along with an attempted murder plot—especially since she just gave me a lot of details about True Mooring."

"I agree."

I drummed my fingers against the table. "What if Tristan knew Carsyn was going to give Olivia the tea and poisoned it without her knowing?"

"That's possible," Cal said.

"And when that plan didn't work, he ran Olivia off the road."

He shook his head. "One problem."

"What?"

"Tristan has a solid alibi for the day Olivia disappeared."

CHAPTER EIGHTEEN

I groaned. "That figures." I longed to bang my head against the conference room table.

Cal ran his fingers through his hair. "Olivia was last seen working out at Fitness Universe, and according to the gym's security cameras, she left around eight. Tristan and Carsyn were serving at Solid Rock from seven in the morning until early evening."

I nodded. "J.T. and I talked to Tristan that afternoon. He could've hired someone to take Olivia out—or there's an accomplice."

"Right." He glanced at his watch. "I'm going over to True Mooring to talk to Tristan Phillips. Want to come?"

"Right now?" I met his eyes. This was a better outcome than I'd imagined.

He shrugged. "Why not? If you promise to let me do the talking, it won't hurt if you observe."

"I promise." I clasped my hands, thrilled that he was willing to trust me. "You're the best."

True Mooring Life Center was located half a mile off the highway, down a county road, in an old limestone church building. Cal turned into the gravel parking lot next to a black Camaro that appeared to be one of the newest models. "Remember to let me do the talking."

"Okay." That wouldn't be easy.

He got out of the car, and I followed him toward the building. A sign labeled *office* pointed to a side entrance, so we stopped next to a glass door. Cal tugged on it, and it was locked. He knocked, and a few seconds later Tristan appeared.

"Welcome to True Mooring Life Center. I'm Tristan." He smiled. "How may I help you?"

Cal flashed his badge. "Detective Cal Perkins, and this is my associate, Georgia Winston."

Associate. I liked that. But I liked pretty much anything he said in his sexy voice.

Tristan stroked his beard as he studied me. "Weren't you the one who came to Solid Rock asking questions about the pastor who was killed?"

"Yes, sir."

"That's a nice Camaro out there," Cal said. "I used to have one like that—older model."

Interesting. He'd never told me that.

"Thanks." Tristan stepped aside and beckoned us in. "Got it this summer, and I need to put it up for the winter, but I'm waiting until the weather takes a turn."

"That's the main reason I traded mine. Not a winter car—especially in Cleveland." He shifted. "I'd like to ask you a few questions about Zach Mishler and Olivia Scott. As you know, Zach was murdered. Now Olivia's missing."

"Yes. I'm happy to help. I had the pleasure of volunteering

with them at Solid Rock Mission. Follow me to the Discovery Room."

We tromped up the red, carpeted steps into what had once been the sanctuary. Tristan had removed the cross, pews, pulpit, and altar and arranged folding chairs in a large circle in the middle of the room. A table next to the wall held stacks of brochures. I searched for anchor-like wall decorations similar to the one in the video, but I didn't see anything.

"Please, sit," Tristan said.

"Yes, sir." We settled onto the metal chairs.

He nodded slowly, and I couldn't read his expression. "I don't know that I'll be able to tell you much more than I already have." He surveyed Cal.

"I won't keep you long, because I'm sure you're busy," Cal said. "A witness told us one of Zach's last words was *anchor*, so we've been looking at all possible connections. The literature from your group talks about the ANCHOR method. Did Zach ever visit your center?"

Tristan shook his head. "No. Definitely not."

"What about Oliva Scott?"

"She visited once or twice with Carsyn Daniels, but she never committed to going through the ANCHOR system."

Assuming Tristan was telling the truth, and Zach hadn't come here, then Olivia could've been the one who shot the video and passed the flash drive on to Zach.

"Tell me more about the ANCHOR system," Cal said.

"I teach a philosophy geared toward making the world a better place."

"How'd you get started?" Cal took out his phone.

He seemed so casual—and friendly.

"Two years ago, I was working as a real estate attorney, but I couldn't find meaning and purpose in my life."

A real estate attorney? *Come on, Cal. Ask about Final Reju-venation.*

"I'd tried church, and it didn't work for me, so I started researching how to help people overcome their struggles without religion. I used the best of modern self-help principles to hone the ANCHOR method."

"Which is?" Cal typed something on his phone.

"The understanding that each of us must find truth within ourselves."

"How many members do you have?" Cal asked.

"Fifty-one." Tristan jiggled his leg up and down. "But we're growing." He walked over to the brochure table and picked up two, which he handed to each of us. "I hope this can help you better understand our philosophy."

"Thank you." I opened the first pamphlet, and it was a dupli-cate of the one Carsyn had given me.

Cal stood. "Thanks for your time."

Why wasn't Cal asking about Final Rejuvenation? Should I? No. I couldn't disrespect him like that. I bit my tongue. He surely had a good reason. I held up the brochure. "How many people have made it to the final level?"

"Only seven, so far. The program is quite rigorous."

"Thanks for the information," I said.

"We have Discovery Sessions for all levels on Wednesday nights and Sunday nights if you wish to join us." Tristan held the door open for us.

"Thanks," I said.

Once we were back in the car and on the road, Cal began whistling, "A Mighty Fortress is Our God."

I sang along in my head and said a silent prayer for the souls of everyone who frequented True Mooring Life Center. "Sorry about earlier. That question just popped out."

He chuckled and turned onto the highway. "It was a good

one. I can't be too mad at you since you managed to stay quiet the rest of the time."

"I'm not sure you understand how big of an accomplishment that is."

"I have a pretty good idea." He winked.

My face burned. "Why didn't you ask about Final Rejuvenation?"

"I wanted to keep him talking, and I can look into that company without asking Tristan."

"He's not hurting for money, since he has a new car."

"It looks that way."

I glanced out the window at the assortment of used vehicles in the lot at Hometown Motors before looking back at Cal. "Speaking of money, Tristan's brother, Jim, gave Mona a huge rock when they got engaged. Maybe he's an accomplice. Or what if Mona's involved too? She told me Olivia was thinking about selling makeup with her company. She'd fit the description of someone Olivia would trust. Mona might've known Olivia liked tea if Zach talked about it. Plus, she's already lied to me about the teenager who died from Jimsonweed poisoning."

"I'll definitely be looking at Tristan and Jim Phillips more closely. I'll do a little digging into Mona Pletcher's life too."

"Good." I made up my mind to talk to Mona as soon as possible.

A few minutes later, we arrived back at the public lot beside the library, and he parked his car next to my truck. He gazed at me. "I'd better get going."

My face flamed as the tension grew between us. Would he *finally* kiss me?

Cal ran his thumb over his shoulder harness. "So'd you ever find a book for Ashley the other day?"

Whoa. A man after my own heart. That distraction move was

straight out of the Georgia Rae Winston Awkwardness Avoidance Handbook.

"Nope. Did you ever find what *you* were looking for?" *Please take the hint.*

"Considering I ran into a beautiful woman? I'd have to say yes."

Are you kidding me right now? "That's sweet."

"Don't worry. I'm sure you'll find the right book." He leaned over and gave me a peck on the cheek.

"I don't know." I stifled a giggle as I opened the car door and leaped out. "It's not easy finding the perfect gift."

"Babe! It's Preston—your favorite twin."

Switching the phone to speaker, I glanced at my watch and dumped a scoopful of food into Gus's dish in my utility room. "You have some answers for me?" I had about twenty minutes to get to rehearsal.

"Yep. What's that *noise?*"

"Sorry. Gus is enjoying his supper." I walked into the kitchen to escape the chomping.

"You need to teach that dog some manners. Just sayin'."

I laughed. "I know. He eats every meal like it's his last. What'd you find?"

"Tristan Phillips owns Final Rejuvenation, LLC."

No surprise there. "Does he have any partners?"

"Nope. But I did a little more digging, and there have been three more decent properties that sold way below market value in the last year or so."

"Let me guess. Final Rejuvenation bought them all?"

"You got it."

CHAPTER NINETEEN

"So, babe. Would you ever live in a tiny house?" Preston asked on Friday morning as he hopped into my truck.

I double checked for no scar—just in case he and his brother had decided to mess with me. *Definitely Preston.*

"Nope. I have too many clothes—and shoes." I slipped my sunglasses on and entered the address of the tiny house compound into the navigation system.

When Austin had finally texted the address the night before, I'd asked both of my stepbrothers to tag along while I drove by and checked it out, but Austin had a closing. Though I would've preferred taking one of my friends, they were all working jobs with no flexibility, and going alone didn't seem too bright.

Especially when Cal didn't know about this unsanctioned look-see.

"Would you ever go tiny?" I turned out of my driveway.

"No." He snorted. "One of my life goals is to own a house bigger than Dad's. Plus, I want a huge outdoor entertaining area. You know—pool, putting green, fire pit, grill." He smirked. "I'll throw some awesome parties with lots of women. Austy and I have a competition going to see who can get his dream house first. I'm definitely going to win. I outsold him last year by a couple hundred thousand."

I fought back a gag. "It's good to have goals." I turned up my satellite radio—which was set to the show tunes channel—and "Anything You Can Do" blasted through the speakers.

No way. "This should be Austin's and your theme song." I sang along.

"Totally." He joined in—with a rather nice baritone.

Even though we had to take several winding, tree-lined roads, it didn't take us more than a few Broadway classics to find the compound.

"That's it." Preston pointed at a gate blocking a gravel drive and a barbed-wire fence.

I slowed the truck and turned down the radio.

"Your destination is on the right," the navigation system said.

"I can't see anything." Preston leaned forward.

I drove by slowly, trying to catch a glimpse of what was down the lane, but there was a bend about a hundred yards down. Even though the trees were bare, they were thick enough to block our view into the woods.

I passed the driveway, parked on the side of the road, and flopped back against the headrest. "Not what I was hoping to find."

"We could go for a hike," Preston said.

I wound a strand of hair around my finger. "It's tempting, but no. Cal's starting to trust me, so I'm not going to betray him like that. It's bad enough that I drove out here without him knowing."

"I get it." He smoothed his dress pants. "I'm not exactly dressed for an adventure in the woods." He looked at his phone. "Plus, I've got to be back at the office in a half hour."

"We tried." I put my truck in drive and started to pull onto the road.

"Hold on, babe. See where that car behind us is going."

I glanced in the rearview mirror at the approaching vehicle. It passed the driveway and stopped beside us. The passenger's side window slid down, so I opened mine.

A gaunt, middle-aged woman, who clearly loved lip fillers to the point of channeling a platypus, leaned over. "Can I help you folks?"

"Do you live here?" I hitched my thumb toward the gate.

"Yes." She tightened the red scarf around her neck.

"Cool." I adopted a perky-casual tone. "One of our friends heard there were a bunch of tiny houses out here. My boyfriend and I *totally* love all those shows on TV about living tiny, and we thought we'd come see in case we ever decide to downsize." I glanced at Preston. "Right, babe?"

Preston coughed. "Right."

Platypus Lips nodded. "It's definitely a simpler way of life. I'm sorry, but I can't invite you in. My neighbors are fierce about their privacy, so we don't give tours."

"Oh, rats." *Who was I right now?* "Tell me this, if you don't mind. Do you ever regret going tiny? I'm afraid I'd be sorry if I got rid of my regular-sized house. I totally like to shop." I giggled.

At least the shopping part wasn't a lie.

She glanced toward the gate. "It takes some adjusting, but it's worth it. I don't miss being overwhelmed with *stuff*." Her tone seemed forced—almost as if she were trying to convince herself. "I'm sure you could do it."

"That's encouraging. I'm Georgia, by the way. This is Preston—my boo." I patted his knee and winked.

The color drained from his face.

"Nice to meet you both." She looked at the gate again. "I have groceries I need to put in my refrigerator."

"Of course. We'll be on our way. Thanks for your time."

She closed the window, backed up her car, and waited at the gate.

It wasn't until we drove down the road that she ventured inside.

"Uh, Georgia?" Preston ran his thumb over his phone.

"Yes." *My boo.*

"If I promise to stop calling you *babe*, will you swear to *never* again refer to me as your *boo*?"

Inside my head, I performed a fully choreographed happy dance, but I managed to keep a straight face. "Deal."

It was a Wildcat Springs Community Church tradition to have carry-in dinners prior to opening night performances, but given Zach's death from poisoning, Ruby and I had decided to modify that ritual. Instead, we'd taken up a collection and hired a caterer to provide the meal.

Pre-show nerves stole my appetite, so after dipping a bit of potato soup and picking up a chocolate chip cookie, I searched for a seat in the café. My gaze fell on Mona, who was sitting alone.

Perfect. I walked over—carefully because I didn't need to slop soup down the front of my tunic. "Mind if I join you?"

"Not at all." She patted the seat beside her, and we ate our supper for a few minutes. "How's the case coming?"

"Slower than I'd like." I leaned closer. "I visited your future-brother-in-law yesterday."

Mona's forehead creased. "Be careful. From what Jim's told me, Tristan's running a cult."

"Yet Jim lets him supervise volunteers at the mission?" I took the last bite of soup.

Mona pressed her lips together. "Jim hoped that by keeping Tristan around, he'd be able to influence him, but he had to let

Tristan go today because he was recruiting. They had an awful fight, and Tristan told Jim he could forget about him being best man at our wedding. I doubt they'll ever speak to each other again."

"I'm sorry." I broke off a piece of cookie. This information sure made Jim appear less guilty. It made Mona look better as well.

"We are too." She shook her head. "Tristan isn't a bad guy. He's had a rough life, and he's just looking for happiness. He wants to help others—however misguided his beliefs may be to us Christians."

"Why has his life been rough?"

"His only son got in over his head gambling, and when he couldn't pay his debt, he was beaten so badly he died. Not long after that, Tristan and his wife divorced."

"That's awful."

"I know. Jim told me the whole story a few days ago. How it inspired Tristan to open a place to help people overcome gambling addictions—"

"Hold the phone. *Anchor* Recovery Center?"

Understanding dawned in her expression. "Yeah, but he sold it about two years ago to start True Mooring. No... Do you think...?" She squeezed the bridge of her nose. "What kind of family am I marrying into?" she murmured.

"Don't panic." I rested my hand on her arm. "Cal will get to the bottom of everything—and I intend to help find the truth."

She raised her head, but her lips trembled. "Thank you."

I stood and tossed my napkin in my empty bowl. "I'm sorry to run, but I'd better get to work." I started to walk away but stopped and looked back. "Leah's going to do great tonight."

"Thanks. I'm one nervous mama. But I shouldn't be. She's wanted to have a starring role in a play ever since she was eight and saw Carsyn play the lead in *Christmas in Paradise*."

I tilted my head as I remembered Carsyn's performance. "I'd forgotten what a good actress Carsyn is."

"Yeah. It's a real shame she isn't using her talent."

"Oh, honey, I'm so proud!" Mom choked me in a bear hug after the opening performance of *A Time Traveler's Christmas* had gone off without a hitch. Not a single problem—even Rob the angel had brilliantly announced the birth of our Savior—in modern English.

"Thanks." The crowd had begun to thin out of the auditorium, and I'd already greeted my friends and met Wanda's son and daughter-in-law. The people who remained stood in clusters around the performers.

"Good work." Dan gave me a high five.

Mom rummaged through her purse for her phone and snapped a picture of me before I could protest. "Let's come back tomorrow and bring friends." She gripped Dan's arm. "Will that be all right? The Sylvans would love this show." She turned to me. "They're our new neighbors. Wonderful couple."

"No problem, dear." Dan truly didn't seem to mind.

"There are still some seats in the center section, so I'll reserve them for you."

"Thanks, sweetie." Mom moved closer and looped her arm through mine. "Let's talk about Christmas."

Oh yay.

"I heard back from Stella today, and Christmas Day works fine for her and Dakota. They're going to be with her side on Christmas Eve." She eyed me. "Are you planning to bring Cal?"

"Um. Well, I don't know. Probably not."

Her forehead creased, and she let go of my arm. "He's welcome. Just like he was at Thanksgiving."

"I know." A dribble of sweat trailed down my back. "We haven't talked about it."

"Don't you think you should?"

I wrapped my arms around my waist. "We'll get to it." I wasn't sure I wanted to subject him to a Winston-Farthing Christmas, though he'd already met my stepbrothers, so how much worse could it be?

I pictured Preston and Austin backing Cal into a corner and playing good cop, bad cop. Yeah. It could get worse all right.

"Jill, ease up. Georgia and Cal will figure it out." Dan issued a smile that I was certain he meant to be reassuring, but, in my present state of mind, felt patronizing.

Mom opened her mouth and then snapped it shut. "No problem. Just let me know so I can set an extra place."

"I will." She prided herself on having a beautiful tablescape at every holiday, and having the proper number of places was crucial to her design. Why hadn't I inherited that talent?

She hugged me again. "See you tomorrow."

I needed to warn Cal—ASAP.

CHAPTER TWENTY

Saturday afternoon, clad in a Christmas sweater with an obnoxious, light-up tree emblazoned on the front, I hefted two shopping bags onto Brandi's dining room table while her Yorkie, Gigi, scuttled around my feet. Brandi had invited me over for our first annual Wrappingpalooza.

I'd done most of my shopping online, and a box of my purchases had arrived the day before, though I didn't have that much to wrap.

Plus, I still didn't have Cal's present. "Ashley's still coming, right?"

"Yep. And I have another reason I wanted us to hang out." She set a plastic tub of ribbons and bows on the table.

"Getting Ashley to talk?" My eyes fell on the plate of Christmas cookies resting on the kitchen counter, so I grabbed an elf cookie and bit off the head.

She touched a finger to her temple. "You're a mind reader."

"No. I'm over her attitude. Whatever she's dealing with needs to get out in the open, so we can help."

The front door opened. "Hey, y'all. I brought plenty of paper, ribbons, and bows." Ashley lugged a plastic container full of wrapping supplies. "The show was awesome last night, by the way."

"Thanks," Brandi and I said in unison.

She set the container down and clapped her hands. "Let's do this."

An hour later, I'd finished my own gifts and had started on Brandi's, which made me realize she had a third motive for Wrappingpalooza. She needed help with the twenty packages for her nieces and nephews.

I'd been shooting Brandi looks at intervals during the last five minutes or so because it was time to begin Operation Make Ashley Talk, or we were going to run out of time before we had to report to church.

Apparently, Brandi expected me to start.

"So, Ash. You seem to be in better spirits this afternoon." I taped some snowmen-printed paper around a Barbie box.

"I am." She attached some red ribbon and eyed the package before selecting a bow.

"Cool." I folded the ends of the paper around the box, caught Brandi's evil eye, and shrugged. If she could do better, then she should've spoken up.

"We're willing to listen." Brandi put a finished package on her stack. "If there's anything you need to talk about."

"Good grief." Ashley sighed and dropped a roll of paper into the container. "I should've told y'all when I moved here, but it never came up, and after a while, it was too weird to talk about." She plopped a LEGO box down on a piece of paper.

What was *it*? My mind spun all sorts of possibilities. "Now we're both thinking the worst."

Ashley looked back and forth between Brandi and me. "Right before I moved here, I was engaged."

Brandi and I exchanged glances.

"I'm sorry." Brandi grasped her hand.

"Who broke it off?" I blurted.

Brandi shot me her teacher look.

I'd never win any points for sensitivity, but there was something to be said for determining context. "I'm sorry."

"I know, Georgia Rae." Ashley sighed. "Jack called it off—on our wedding day—because he'd met someone else." She yanked a piece of tape from the dispenser. "When I was home for Thanksgiving, I ran into Jack and his wife...and their baby boy."

My stomach flopped. "Ouch."

Ashley swallowed. "Yeah. I didn't want it to affect me, but it did. The Sunday I backed out of hosting small group was the anniversary of our engagement. Seeing them so happy after Jack cheated on me... It's not fair." She snipped a piece of ribbon. "I've never dated anyone seriously—since Jack. A dinner and movie with a guy here and there—and that's it." She pawed through the bow container and selected a burgundy one that she slapped on the box. "I haven't acted like it, but I'm having trouble trusting again."

All this time she'd pretended to be more open to relationships than Brandi and me when she'd been faking it. Yet how could I be mad? I wasn't the type who enjoyed spilling my deepest, darkest secrets.

"That makes sense," Brandi said. "I'll pray that when the time's right, you'll meet a guy who's worth trusting."

"Same here."

"Thank you." Ashley nodded.

"Thanks for telling us," Brandi said.

"Yeah. I know that wasn't easy." I picked up a walkie-talkie set for one of Brandi's nephews and peeled off the sticky note she'd used to label it.

We wrapped for a while with only the sounds of ripping tape and scissors slicing paper punctuating the silence.

"Ash, when you're ready, what about dating J.T.? He's a pretty great guy." I grinned. "Don't tell him I said that." In my head, I started singing "Matchmaker" from *Fiddler on the Roof.*

"I know he is." Ashley met my eyes. "I wouldn't rule him out, but he only thinks of me as a friend—which is fine. I don't want to make things awkward at small group."

"I get it." I'd talk to J.T. soon and let him know there was hope —if he was willing to be patient.

Ashley finished the final present in her pile and put it aside. "How's the murder investigation coming?" She took an unwrapped gift from Brandi's stack.

"My current theory is that Tristan Phillips might be guilty of cheating people out of money—and real estate." I gave them a summary of my visit to True Mooring Life Center with Cal and my visit with Platypus Lips at the tiny house compound. "Olivia visited True Mooring with Carsyn. I think she suspected what Tristan was up to, so he used Carsyn to get the poisoned tea leaves to Olivia. Except, instead of making the tea, she passed it onto Zach."

"Creepy," Brandi said. "You really think Carsyn's in on it?"

"I'm not sure. It's possible Tristan poisoned the tea without Carsyn knowing." I ran my hand over the table to clear off scraps of wrapping paper. "Plus, there's an accomplice who may've caused Olivia to run off the road into the Sloans' pond. Since they didn't find her body, I wonder if she escaped but the accomplice caught her and finished her off." I tossed the paper bits in the trash.

Ashley tapped her nails against the counter.

"What're you thinking, Ash?" Brandi asked.

"I know someone from work who might be able to help." Ashley looked at me. "What time do you have to be at church?"

I glanced at the clock on Brandi's wall. "I need to leave in about a half hour."

She took her phone out of her pocket and began texting. "Let's see if he's available to video chat."

Ten minutes later, her phone rang. "Hey, Choi, how can I help?"

Ashley moved her phone, so I was in camera range. "Steve, this is my friend, Georgia."

"Nice to meet you." Steve slid his dark-framed glasses up on his large nose and waved.

"Hey." I hoped my shock didn't show in my expression. He was one of the people from the secret video recording.

Ashley turned back to her phone. "Yesterday, when you told me that you almost got sucked into a cult. What was the name?"

"True Mooring Life Center." His eyes widened. "Your friend having the same experience? If so, run—fast."

"No, no. I just have a few questions," I said. "Anything you can tell me about the place would be great."

"Sure." Steve shook his head. "Basically, the guy at True Mooring preys on vulnerable people."

"How'd you meet him?" I asked.

"I was volunteering at Solid Rock Mission, so I could connect with people in the community, and Tristan was there. At first, I thought he was a quirky dude who'd be fun to hang out with, so when he asked if I wanted to shoot pool and have a few beers, I said yes. Halfway through the evening, he started in with a spiel —which sounded good. I mean, I *was* lonely. I moved from Florida to Richardville for my job. No wife or kids. So I decided to check out his Discovery Session one Wednesday night."

"What was it like?" I asked.

"Solid self-help principles—at least in the Arise level. I was hoping to break my nail-biting habit." He held up his hand with his gnawed off nails facing me. "Worked for a while. Then

Tristan started asking for money before I could be promoted to the Negate level. When I wasn't willing to pony up a thousand bucks to move on, Tristan lost interest in me. But I'd already decided he was a con artist."

"Did you report him?"

"No." Steve glanced away. "I probably should've, but if people want to waste their money on mumbo-jumbo to make themselves feel better, it's none of my business. Besides, I had this feeling it'd be best to keep my mouth shut and move on."

"Why?" There had to be something specific that Steve wasn't telling me.

He looked down for a few seconds. "One night, I went to the bathroom and overheard a guy threatening some woman that if she didn't meet her recruitment quota, there'd be serious consequences. She was crying."

Ashley drew in a sharp breath, and Brandi pursed her lips and shook her head.

Though I agreed with my friends' reactions, I didn't dare act judgmental if I wanted to keep Steve talking. "Any idea who the guy was?"

"No—it wasn't Tristan. I'd have recognized his voice, since he sounds like a radio announcer."

"Did you ever meet Tristan's brother Jim when you volunteered at Solid Rock?" I asked.

"Yeah. But it wasn't him. This guy's voice was higher pitched than Jim's or Tristan's—not squeaky or anything—just an average dude voice."

"Did you see the woman?

"No, but he called her Carsyn."

I bit my lip. "A couple more questions. Give me a second." Using my phone, I went to the church website and opened up Zach's picture. I held up my phone. "Did you ever see this man at your meetings?"

"No."

I switched to my news app and found Olivia Scott's picture. "How about her?"

"Yep. She was definitely in my Arise group."

CHAPTER TWENTY-ONE

On the way to the church, I was a good girl and left a message with Cal about everything I'd learned from Steve. Clearly, Tristan had a partner, and I now had doubts about it being Carsyn—unless she'd been coerced.

As soon as I entered the church's greenroom on Saturday night, the tension in the air smacked me in the face. Ruby sprawled on the couch with the back of her hand to her forehead while Mona tended to her. Cast and choir members stood in small clusters, whispering. Our leads, Sharon and Leah, who were already in costume, swarmed me as soon as I entered.

"Rob's sick." Sharon buttoned her lab coat. Goggles resting on her head completed her transformation into Millie.

I let my purse slide off my shoulder. "How sick?"

Leah held out a phone, and I took it. "He sent this to Ruby a few minutes ago."

In hospital with food poisoning. I'm out.

Poor Rob. I mentally reviewed the people in the show who

could replace him at a moment's notice, and there weren't many. At least our leads were well. "Don't worry, everybody. The show will go on."

"Who'll play the angel?" one of the men asked, almost as if he hoped I'd cast him. But his oversized belly disqualified him from fitting into the costume—and harness.

"We'll figure something out." I took a deep breath and tiptoed over to Ruby, which halfway to the couch struck me as funny, and I had to choke back a giggle. Mona got up and walked away as I knelt beside Ruby. "It's Georgia."

She shot up as if waking from a nightmare, and I performed an evasive maneuver to miss her flailing arm. "This is simply a *disaster*. I've called other problems disasters, but this time I mean it. What'll we *do*? What if more people have food poisoning from our meal? I thought we'd be safe using a caterer." She buried her face in her hands. "Last night's show was too perfect. I *tried* to be thankful, but I had this *horrible* feeling that something was about to go wrong."

I started to reassure her but realized that might be a mistake. She had a valid point. One bad dish could take out most of the cast. "Let's not assume it was something Rob ate while he was here. I'm feeling okay. Are there any other messages from cast members?" I handed over her phone.

She lifted her head and checked. "No."

"Good. Then we just need to recast the angel."

"You." Ruby gripped my hand. "You're the only one I trust. Besides, the harness will fit you because you and Rob are close in size."

Nothing like having my build compared to a guy's. "But—"

"We should probably have a man play the part, but we're desperate, and you're pretty enough to pull it off. Besides, I've already had to compromise by having a doll play Baby Jesus." She flopped back against the couch.

"But...the choir?"

She sat up. "You'll direct as normal until just before it's time to announce Jesus's birth. Then, you'll go backstage and get hooked up. After you proclaim the arrival of our messiah, you'll lead the choir as they sing 'Behold.'"

"While suspended from the ceiling." I couldn't let Cal see me in such a ridiculous position.

Ruby clasped her hands. "It's brilliant, don't you think?"

"I don't—"

"We'll make sure you're low enough for the choir to see." She patted my shoulder and stood. "Crisis averted. Let's go practice, so you can get used to flying!"

An hour later in the chapel after warm-ups, I knew what my face must've looked like when Ruby had proposed her solution to the angel problem because the choir had gaped at me when I'd explained my angel/choir director role.

Seven out of thirty-three choir members had texted to say they were experiencing various levels of food poisoning. In addition, we'd recast a shepherd and the innkeeper. The general consensus was the macaroni salad had been the culprit.

Brandi raised her hand, and I nodded at her. "And we'll be able to see you?" We'd been friends long enough for me to know she was dying to say more. Not to mention the motherly side of her probably had concerns about me hanging ten feet above the stage.

I cleared my throat. "Ruby stood on the risers in several different places and told me she could see. Just look up when it's time for cut offs. Otherwise, don't strain your necks." I tried to smile confidently, but my wobbly effort landed somewhere between uncertain and terrified. "Take a break, and be ready to go onstage in twenty."

A few people whispered to each other, and I could only imagine the things they were saying about Ruby—and me.

Brandi walked up to me. "If I weren't afraid of heights, I'd be willing to step in." She patted her curls. "I could be angelic."

"You'd be more convincing than me." I'd considered using fear of heights as an excuse, but more than one person in this program had probably driven by my farm and seen me working at the top of one of my grain bins, so that excuse was dead on arrival. "But I wouldn't wish this contraption on you." I patted my waist, though my angel robe hid the harness. "The leg straps are pretty snug on my thunder thighs."

"Are you *kidding* me?" Ruby shrieked from offstage.

"Now what?" I muttered.

Brandi and I hurried into the greenroom while I prayed silently that we hadn't lost any more cast members to food poisoning.

Ruby held up a box of chocolate Teddy Grahams for everyone who'd gathered in a semicircle around her. "People. I just. Replaced these." She shook the box, demonstrating that it was empty. "Does *no one* care that I get low blood sugar?"

Brandi and I exchanged glances.

"I've kept snacks in my desk for *years*, and it's only been for *this* show that I've had problems with food and water vanishing!" she shouted.

No way.

Vanishing food. Missing water. And what about the scratching noises?

It couldn't be. Could it?

"Be right back," I whispered to Brandi. I had no intention of spouting off my theory and having my best friend thinking I belonged in the looney bin.

Hoisting up my angel tunic, I moved in a run-limp combo out of the greenroom and down the hall to the old church building. I hustled down the basement stairs, and a sour smell—much stronger than the usual mustiness—whacked my nostrils.

"Merciful heavens." I clasped my hand over my nose and mouth.

A horrid retching noise came from the restroom, and I pushed through the door. A woman wearing work-out clothes sprawled in front of the toilet. Slowly, as if it took great effort, she turned to face me.

Olivia Scott.

CHAPTER TWENTY-TWO

"Have you been here since Zach died?" I blinked at her, not quite believing my wacky theory had been spot on.

"Yes. Right after some crazy person ran me off the road." Olivia choked back a sob and rubbed her red eyes.

"I'll go get help." Thanks to Ruby's prohibition on phones, mine was stowed in my purse in the greenroom.

"No. Don't!" She braced herself against the toilet and struggled to rise to her knees.

"Why not?"

"He's after me."

"Tristan Phillips?"

"Yes." She lunged toward the toilet and vomited again.

I knelt beside her and held her ponytail out of the way. Clearly, she hadn't found much to eat. Her black leggings, that had probably fit snugly two weeks ago, were baggy. "Did you happen to eat macaroni salad last night?"

"Yeah." Olivia hung her head. "When I found the leftovers from the dinner, I couldn't believe it. Everything tasted so good—

especially after living on Christmas cookies and Teddy Grahams."

I patted her arm. "You have food poisoning—like about ten other people on our cast."

Her shoulders slumped. "I hoped that's all it was, but with Zach—" She covered her face. "He was really special."

"I'm so sorry." I tore off a wad of toilet paper and handed it to her. "Why are you hiding instead of going to the police?"

She drew a shuddering breath. "Partly because I'd be their number one suspect. I gave Zach the tea, and he texted on Friday morning to tell me he loved it. I swear I didn't know it was poisoned. Obviously, it was meant for me, and I've been wishing over and over I'd been the one to drink it."

"Where'd you get it?"

"Carsyn Daniels. For my birthday. But the tea had peppermint, which I hate, so I passed it on to Zach because he likes—I mean *liked*—it." More tears spilled over. "I just can't believe she tried to kill me."

I closed my eyes. "Did Carsyn hand it to you?"

"No. That's the thing. The tea was in my massage room at work, but her name was on the tag. It was sitting with all of my other presents from the girls at work. We always get each other gifts on our birthdays."

"When was your birthday?"

"November 21—the Tuesday before Thanksgiving."

I chewed my lower lip as I tried to figure out Olivia's logic about hiding. "I understand why you're scared, but why didn't you go to the police and explain?"

"I already did." Her chin trembled.

"What?"

"Not about the tea. About the scam at True Mooring." She swiped her hand across her cheek.

"The one where Tristan Phillips is manipulating people out

of their money and property."

She refused to meet my eyes. "Yes."

I put my hands on her shoulders. "Olivia. I can help. I've been investigating."

She wrenched away and vomited again. When she finished, she handed me an empty water bottle. "Please fill this first."

I put water in the bottle, and when I gave it to her, she swished water in her mouth and spat in the toilet a few times.

"Okay." She took a deep breath. "The Monday before Zach was killed, I went to the sheriff's department and talked to Detective Kimball, but I could tell he didn't take me seriously." She sipped her water. "I told him I suspected Tristan was manipulating level six members at True Mooring Life Center into selling their property to his corporation for cheap as a condition of attaining full Rejuvenation status."

"How'd you know if you only attended the first level meetings?"

"I felt weird after the first meeting and thought Carsyn was getting in over her head, but I probably would've let it go if it hadn't been for my massage client, Jody Chatfield." She rinsed her mouth again. "For a couple of years, all Jody could talk about was building her dream home on a ten-acre property that her aunt had left her." She turned away from the toilet. "Not long after I'd been to True Mooring with Carsyn, Jody came in and told me she'd sold her colonial in town and had given up on building the dream home. Instead, she was going to put a tiny house on the land she'd inherited, and several other people were moving their tiny houses there too. I asked her why and she said the ANCHOR system had made her view life differently, and blah, blah, blah."

"Does Jody Chatfield have lips that've been overly injected?" I asked.

"Oh yeah. Not a good look, right?" Olivia sniffed. "I got to talking about it with Zach since we were dating, and he'd heard his friend who sells real estate say how a woman with big lips had sold her house for way below market value. We figured out it was Jody."

I twisted a strand of hair around my finger. "I went to the tiny house compound yesterday and talked to Jody, and she seemed nervous. Not at all like someone who was truly happy about downsizing."

"Right. She's totally materialistic. It doesn't make sense that she'd give up on building her dream house."

"That's when you went back to True Mooring with a hidden camera and snooped in Tristan's office to find evidence."

She nodded. "Until he caught me. I tried to say I was looking for the bathroom, but he didn't believe me, so I got out of there fast."

"You gave Zach a copy of the video, the picture of the tiny-house compound, and the real estate listing for safekeeping?"

"Yes. And I gave copies to Detective Kimball." She nodded. "Friday morning, I was driving home from Fitness Universe, when an SUV ran me off the road and into Sloan's Pond. I lost my phone and my laptop with the evidence in the wreck."

"Was the SUV white?"

"Yeah. How'd you know?"

"Someone tried a similar trick with me." Except the driver hadn't managed to run me off the road.

"I barely got out of my car, and when I did, the SUV was gone. I was afraid to call the police." She wrapped her arms around her torso. "It was *after* I told Detective Kimball my suspicions that I almost got killed? Pretty sketchy."

Sketchy indeed. What if Detective Kimball had tailgated me with the hope that Cal would have a change of heart about me poking around in the case? Then, through Cal, he could keep track of what I knew.

I fought a shiver, but I had to keep Olivia talking because time was running out before curtain. "After the crash, you walked to the church."

"I was trying to get to Zach, but the ambulance was here loading him." She pressed her fist to her mouth for a moment and closed her eyes. Then she dropped her hand in her lap. "While I figured out what to do, I snuck inside the church, dried off, and changed into a white robe I found on the floor in the hall. It looked like the one you've got on. I hid, and later, I overheard someone say Zach had died from poisoning. I searched for the flash drive with the evidence because he told me he'd hidden it at church. After the first night, I figured out no one came down here, so I stayed. In the middle of the night, I used the shower in the restrooms over by the baptistery, and I did laundry in the washer and dryer." She took another sip of water.

I considered everything she'd told me. "Tristan's running a scam—which I already suspected. Marvin Kimball is probably in on it, which is new information. What about Tristan's brother, Jim? Or Jim's fiancée Mona Pletcher? Or Carsyn?"

Olivia rested her head against the metal partition. "I don't know about Jim or Mona, but my gut feeling is Carsyn was set up. Why would she put her name on the tea if she knew it was poisoned? I think Tristan poisoned it after she bought it. Since they're dating, he would've had access to it."

"I thought the same thing," I said. "I have a witness who attended a session at True Mooring and overheard Carsyn being threatened that she had to meet her recruitment quota or face consequences. The witness said the man doing the threatening had a higher pitched voice—not deep like Jim's and Tristan's. He surely would've said if it was gravelly like Detective Kimball's." I tightened my fingers into a fist. "Which means there's a third person involved."

CHAPTER TWENTY-THREE

"You have to tell Detective Perkins what you know." I shifted my legs because the harness straps were digging into my skin.

"No way." Olivia's eyes widened.

"Cal's trustworthy."

She picked at the wrapper on her water bottle.

"Georgia? Are you okay? It's five minutes until curtain!" Ruby's shrill voice reverberated through the basement.

Terror flitted across Olivia's face, and she jumped up, steadying herself against the stall.

"Stay hidden. I'll find a way to help," I whispered as I stood. I darted out of the restroom and blocked the door. "Sorry." I hitched my thumb over my shoulder. "Don't go in there. Pre-show nerves do a number on my colon." I pressed my hand to my abdomen.

Ruby grimaced. "We need you to hurry."

I followed her upstairs into the greenroom. When a cast member intercepted her, I slipped into the wings and scanned the audience, hoping to find Cal quickly. He wasn't in the seat I'd reserved for him in the fifth row. Nor was he anywhere in the auditorium.

I spotted Carsyn holding Tristan's hand in the front row. Mom and Dan were sitting with Aunt Janie, Uncle Todd, J.T. and their neighbors. Preston and Austin had decided to show up and were sitting on the far right. Not the greatest seats, but that's what they got for waiting until the last minute. Otherwise, I could've put them in the center with Mom and Dan.

I scanned the room again, hoping to see Cal coming in the back, but he must've been running late. "Cal, where are you?" I muttered as I darted toward the corner of the greenroom where I'd stored my purse. I found my phone in the bottom of my handbag and started to send a text.

"Georgia!" Running toward me, Ruby pointed at my phone. "Put that away. The choir's waiting for you to lead them out."

"One minute."

"Not acceptable." Ruby tried to snatch my phone, but I held it over her reach, and she jumped like a Chihuahua trying to reach a bone.

"Ruby, back off!" I shouted in a tone that was anything but angelic. At least I hadn't said all the words that'd been pinging in my head.

She huffed and stalked away, muttering something about missing Jessica Myers and disrespectful millennials.

Whatever. There were bigger problems than her feelings. I typed a message to Cal as fast as I could.

I found Olivia Scott. Help!!!!!

I made sure the message sent before silencing it. Then I tucked it into my bra—a practice I'd never done—or intended to do again, but it wasn't like my angel robe had pockets.

The opening music was beginning as I scurried to the front of the line. Taking a deep breath, I led the choir out to the risers on stage left and surveyed the audience. Cal was sitting in his seat and looking down. My phone vibrated.

Once the choir was in place, I led them through the opening number, "Hustle-Bustle." When the lights dimmed, I bolted into the wings and checked Cal's reply.

Where?

I didn't want to give up her location until he understood Detective Kimball was dirty. Though I trusted him completely, I didn't want to inadvertently put Olivia in danger if Cal called for backup.

Marvin Kimball is a dirty cop. Meet me backstage.

I peeked from behind the curtain and saw Cal get up and walk toward the exit. Leah was now in the middle of her solo, "More Than Santa," which meant I had about a minute until the choir sang again.

We'd have to wait until next break.

Leah finished, and as the crowd broke into applause, I took my place in front of the choir and caught Brandi's wide-eyed glance.

"Pray," I mouthed.

She gave me a thumbs up.

Taking a deep breath, I led the choir through "Step into History," which was Millie's response to Leah's questions about the real meaning of Christmas. During the song, they got into the sleigh time machine and arrived at their first stop—Judea—where Mary was visiting her cousin Elizabeth.

When I darted into the wings, Cal stood in the greenroom

doorway. I rushed over, grabbed his arm, and yanked him inside, trying to ignore the harness's pinching straps.

"Olivia Scott reported a possible extortion scheme going on at True Mooring Life Center to Marvin Kimball on the Monday before Zach was killed."

He gaped at me. "Are you serious? Marvin never mentioned that to me." He ran his fingers through his hair.

"That's because he's in on it. I think he's been helping Tristan Phillips dig up dirt on people, so they'll surrender their money and property more easily. Then Tristan gives him a cut."

Cal shook his head. "No way. I've seen Marvin's house—and cars. He's not living above his means."

"What if he's hiding the money?"

"I doubt it. Last week his debit card got declined when we were eating lunch, and I had to pick up the tab."

"Then Tristan must be blackmailing him for some reason. Plus, there has to be a third person involved." I told him about what Ashley's coworker, Steve, had witnessed.

Cal flattened his lips.

I rested my hand on his arm. "Please. I know you don't want to think that about your partner, but the day Zach was killed, a white SUV ran Olivia off the road—a few days *after* she reported Tristan to Marvin. Plus, the Jimsonweed tea was meant for her, but since it had peppermint and she hates that flavor, she gave it to Zach." I lowered my voice. "The tea was a birthday gift that had Carsyn Daniel's name on the tag, but Olivia never saw Carsyn put it in her massage room at work. It just appeared there with all the other gifts."

Elizabeth and Mary's song, "Blessed is She," was winding down, so I had to be back on stage in about five seconds.

Mary hit the final note in her beautiful soprano.

"Got to go," I whispered. "One more song before intermission."

"But—"

I scurried back on stage as the lights came up on Joseph. For the next three minutes, I focused all my energy on "Can It Be?" because this piece about Joseph learning that Mary was expecting Jesus was the most difficult in the show. At the song's conclusion, the curtain closed, and I gimped over to Cal.

"Let's go. I've got ten minutes." I grabbed his hand and dragged him into the hallway. Dodging the shepherds and children dressed as sheep, I led him to the old church building. I glanced over my shoulder to make sure no one had followed us and we were alone.

"She's been hiding here?" Skepticism filled his tone as we took the narrow staircase into the basement.

"Yep." I pushed open the ladies' restroom door, but the space was empty.

Cal opened the men's room door, and we found only a toilet, urinal, and sink.

"Olivia?" I whispered. "It's Georgia."

We quickly checked the closets and each of the Sunday school rooms.

Olivia had vanished.

CHAPTER TWENTY-FOUR

"I told her to stay here." I scowled and put my hands on my hips.

"Maybe someone else found her first." Cal headed for the stairs. "I'm going to find Carsyn and Tristan."

"I'm sorry." I trailed behind. "I was afraid if you came down here without me, then Olivia would get spooked. She's terrified of law enforcement."

He set his jaw. "We'll find her."

When we came to the new part of the building, Cal disappeared into the café where audience members were milling around. I returned to the greenroom, just in time to lead the choir on stage. I scanned the auditorium, and Carsyn's and Tristan's seats were empty. I hoped Cal had found them.

"Are you okay?" Brandi mouthed.

I shook my head.

Once everyone was in place, the choir began singing "O Little Town of Bethlehem" while Mary and Joseph approached the inn, looking for shelter. Millie and Leah watched the action unfold on stage right.

When the song ended, I tried to piece the case together while Mary and Joseph—Doug and Ella—walked to the stable.

Doug.

My stomach clenched when I remembered what Mona had told me about Tristan selling Anchor Recovery Center. What if Doug was the third person? What if Tristan knew about his gambling problem—or debts—and was using that to manipulate him into helping with his extortion scheme?

Doug's tenor voice was pitched higher than Jim's or Tristan's, and he might've known about Olivia's and Zach's love of tea. But how would he have gotten the tea to Olivia?

I fought back the emotions that battled to display themselves on my face. Not now. Not onstage. I didn't want to think that any of this evil was possible in my little hometown. But this was the same place where my daddy had been murdered. Where Tara Fullerton had been killed. A small town didn't shield us from the evil in the world—it only lulled us into pretending we were safe.

Mary moaned in pain as the stage lights faded. Jesus was born during a scene change, so we didn't traumatize any small children in the audience. It was time for me to lead the choir in the "Away in a Manger" medley, so I steeled my focus while Mary and Joseph cuddled the Baby Jesus doll instead of their dear Lyla.

When the choir finished singing and the stage lights darkened, I moved into the wings—because it was time for me to proclaim our Savior's birth. The shepherds and sheep children hurried into place with a chorus of footsteps, whispers, and shushing.

I swiped my halo from the prop table and stuck it on my head.

"Ready?" Alex, the stage hand, held the wires in his hand.

"Yep." I turned so he could clip them onto the harness through the openings in my robe. I shifted as the straps pulled taut against my legs and hips. I'd have to give Olivia a call for a massage when things calmed down.

Olivia. Massage.

Why was that bugging me?

The pulley system gently lifted me ten feet off the ground, and the curtain opened as the orchestra started the next song. I slapped on an angelic expression.

Inspire Salon & Spa.

That was it. The third person wasn't Doug—it was Pete Litchfield.

Focus. I held out my arms. "Fear not. For behold, I bring you—"

Two things happened at once.

First, my eyes fell on Olivia, who'd donned a biblical costume and had taken a place with the choir on the left edge of the front row—almost in the wings.

Second, Pete Litchfield crept along the back wall toward the auditorium's right exit.

I drew in a deep breath. "For behold, I bring you the truth about Zach Mishler's murder."

CHAPTER TWENTY-FIVE

P ete Litchfield froze.

My eyes fell on Preston and Austin, who were sitting right next to the door. "Preston, Austin—stop him." I pointed at Pete, and my stepbrothers launched out of their seats as the house lights blinked on.

I swayed above the stage.

Pete's wife Winnie jumped up and tried to use her girth to hinder them, but Austin hadn't been on an offensive line for nothing. He blocked her so Preston could sneak around.

Preston tackled Pete and wrenched his hands behind his back.

A gasp swept over the audience, and people stood to see the commotion. Carsyn and Tristan stood at the back of the auditorium next to Cal, who held his phone to his ear and looked back and forth between Tristan and the scuffle.

"Get your hands off my husband." Winnie leaped toward Preston's back, but Austin took her down.

"Don't touch me!" she bellowed.

A sheriff's deputy raced into the auditorium, and Cal pointed to Preston, Austin, and Pete. Clearly, he didn't intend to leave Tristan, which was a smart move.

I had to forge ahead before Ruby—or someone else—tried to silence me. "Let me explain." I motioned for everyone to be seated and waited for the crowd to hush. "Zach's death was accidental, because the poison wasn't intended for him."

Ruby stood on her seat in the auditorium and waved her arms. "Stop her," she wailed. "She's ruining my show!"

A murmur of confusion rippled through the room.

I held up a hand. "Zach was dating Olivia Scott, and they both liked tea. When Olivia received a new blend for her birthday, she gave it to Zach because it contained peppermint—which she hated. She didn't know the tea contained poisonous Jimsonweed seeds. The tea had a tag from Carsyn Daniels, but—"

"How dare you!" Ruby charged on stage. "You have no right to ruin my show—and my daughter's reputation."

Pastor Mark, who was filling in for a sick shepherd, rushed over and put his arm around her. "Let her finish."

"The tea didn't come from Carsyn. Pete Litchfield, Olivia's neighbor, scheduled a massage with her on her birthday and placed the package of tea with Olivia's other gifts in the massage room at the salon. He put Carsyn's name on the tag, hoping Olivia would make and drink the tea without question. When she died, everyone would blame Carsyn." I scanned the crowd. "I'm sure everyone's wondering why Pete would want to poison Olivia Scott."

"If you're going to ruin my show, you'd better tell us it had nothing to do with my baby," Ruby shouted.

This statement drew a few nervous chuckles from the audience and the choir. The other shepherds began ushering the sheep-children off stage. Olivia pulled her head covering tighter but nodded, as if she wanted me to continue.

The deputy reached Pete, took him from Preston, and hand-cuffed him.

"Olivia stumbled on an extortion scheme involving Pete. Not long after she attended a Discovery Session at True Mooring Life Center with Carsyn, one of Olivia's massage clients, Jody Chatfield, talked about how she'd given up building her dream house in favor of living in a tiny house. That seemed weird to Olivia, and when she learned Jody was involved with True Mooring, she decided to investigate, since she'd gotten funny vibes during her own visit. Zach helped because of his expertise in real estate. After they did some digging, Olivia suspected the leader of True Mooring, Tristan Phillips, was extorting money and property from group members and investing it in his company, Final Rejuvenation, LLC. Rejuvenate is the last stage of the ANCHOR program at True Mooring Life Center—and is the reason why *anchor* was one of Zach's last words. Olivia saved the evidence on a flash drive and gave it to Detective Marvin Kimball with the hope that he'd investigate further. Instead, he immediately informed Tristan Phillips and Pete Litchfield."

A murmur rippled through the crowd again. In the back, Carsyn covered her face with her hands, and Cal grabbed Tristan's arms.

"I've always said you can't trust cops," Bobbi Sue Miller shouted from the center section.

For once, her paranoia wasn't wrong. "Tristan once owned Anchor Recovery Center and knew Pete Litchfield had a gambling problem. After Tristan sold the center to start True Mooring, he manipulated Pete into helping him extort money from True Mooring members in exchange for paying off his gambling debts—and I suspect he did the same for Detective Kimball, who probably used his detective skills to dig up dirt on members."

The audience turned toward Pete, who squirmed in the

deputy's grip. Austin and Preston stood on each side of them—clearly ready to provide backup.

"Don't say a word, Pete," Winnie shouted. "They'll use it against you. We'll prove none of this is true. That busybody farmer-detective is just making up stories."

Pete hung his head as the deputy led him out. Poor Winnie.

I took a deep breath and ignored the throbbing pain in my legs. "To protect their scheme, the men came up with the plan to kill Olivia. Tristan knew that Jimsonweed was poisonous because his niece's boyfriend died from ingesting it earlier this year. As Olivia's neighbor, Pete was aware Olivia liked tea and used his friendly relationship with her to his advantage. A few days later, when the poison tea scheme didn't work, Detective Kimball stole an SUV and ran her off the road into Sloan's Pond—but she survived and has been hiding in our church basement ever since."

Olivia pushed down her head covering and stepped out of the choir, and the audience buzzed. Two more deputies raced into the auditorium and took Tristan from Cal.

Alex, the stagehand, lowered me to the floor, and when he unhooked the wires, I sank down, my robe pooling around me.

After the excitement, Pastor Mark and Ruby decided that finishing the show was futile, and Pastor Mark made a quick announcement to anyone who was listening, encouraging them to return for a Sunday evening performance.

Ruby would probably never forgive me, but I was totally fine with that. Word on the street was that Jessica Myers was on the mend, so she could have her job back.

I was sitting on the couch in the greenroom trying to catch my breath when Preston and Austin rushed in. I held up my hand for a high five. "Nice work, sidekicks."

They each slapped my hand.

"That was one of the most awesome things I've ever seen," Preston said. "You were like the Angel of Truth."

"Like a superhero in a movie." Austin crossed his arms.

I nearly choked on my next words, but they needed to be said. "I couldn't have done it without you guys."

They beamed. "We know."

Mom and Dan joined us. "Are you okay, sweetie?" Mom sat down next to me, removing my halo and stroking my hair.

"Yeah. My heartrate still hasn't slowed down to normal."

Carsyn Daniels stood in the doorway, and I got up. "Excuse me." I made a beeline for her.

She hugged me as soon as I reached her. "Thank you." She stepped back. "I was so scared, and didn't know what to do, because I was in over my head at True Mooring. I'm sorry I tried to recruit you and Rob, but I had to keep up appearances. Tristan was after me to talk to you both. I even had to record our conversations as proof." She covered her face with her hands. "I'm so, so, sorry for dragging Olivia and Zach into this."

I hugged her again.

She pulled away, turmoil brewing in her eyes. "Do you think God could ever forgive me?"

A time to speak. "Absolutely. He can forgive anything." I rested my hand on her shoulder. "He's just waiting for you to ask."

Sunday afternoon, I sat at the piano playing through my childhood hymnal. After everything that'd happened, it was cheap therapy. Gus napped on the floor beside me. I was in the middle of "Come, Thou Long-Expected Jesus" when my doorbell rang.

The dog charged ahead of me and paced in front of the door until I answered.

"Hey, Cal." I motioned for him to come in.

"How's the Angel of Truth?"

I giggled. "You've been talking to Preston and Austin."

"You have two loyal sidekicks for life. They were arguing over what their superhero names should be when I talked to them last night."

I shut the door. "Did you arrest Marvin?"

"Last night." Cal slipped off his jacket. "He had huge gambling debts, and Tristan paid them off. In exchange, Marvin helped him manipulate members into selling their houses to Final Rejuvenation for below market value—or just donating large sums of cash. He was also the one who broke into your house and stole your laptop because he knew you were out on a date with me."

"Will I get it back?"

"Eventually. Unfortunately for you, it's evidence."

I sighed. At least my files were backed up offsite.

He followed me into the living room. "This whole case turns my stomach." He shook his head and then sat down on the sofa. "You ready for tonight's performance?"

I perched next to him and did a mental facepalm when I realized we'd both passed under the mistletoe—without noticing.

Good grief. We deserved each other.

I pulled my gaze away from the useless decoration. "I can't wait to get it over with and move on. Rob's feeling better, so I don't have to give a repeat performance as the angel." My legs and hips couldn't handle another night in the harness.

"I doubt Ruby would've let you." Cal's eyes twinkled.

"Very true."

Gus moved over to sit beside Cal, and he patted the dog's head. "So. I've had a little dilemma with Christmas coming."

Had he been struggling with a gift for me? *Life Lesson #64: Always play it cool.* "Really?"

"Since I've not dealt with the divorced parents thing before, I've been trying to figure out where I should go for Christmas. My mom's or my dad's new place in Florida? I've been reading books on how to cope with divorced parents, which is kind of nerdy, I know."

"Not at all." No wonder he hadn't wanted to tell me what books he'd gotten at the library that day. I'd been so worried about his gift that I'd missed his struggle over Christmas. *Stupid, stupid, stupid!* "What'd you decide?"

"My sister figured it out. She refuses to pick, so she's going to stay home and make her own memories with her family."

"Where does that leave you?"

"I'm going to take some time off and help my dad move to Florida in a week, but for Christmas I'll be back here working." He chuckled. "I'm willing to take one for the team if it helps out some other guys with families."

"All day? Because if you'd like to hang out with my family and me in the evening..."

"I'd love that." He reached for my hand and gave it a squeeze. "Now. Did I hear you playing the piano when I arrived?"

"Yes."

"How about a little concert?"

I stood. "What're you in the mood for?"

"Let's see." He strolled over to the wooden music stand next to my piano and flipped through the books. "The carving on this stand is phenomenal, by the way."

"Thanks. Daddy made it for my fifteenth birthday." He'd surrounded an inlaid *G* with curlicues.

"How about this one?" He handed me a book of show tunes open to "Till There Was You" from *The Music Man.*

My face warmed. "Of course."

I settled on the piano bench—and Cal took a seat beside me.

I drew in a steadying breath. How on earth was I supposed to concentrate on the music with him so close by? I glanced up at him. "Just so you know, I haven't played this one for a while, so it might be a little rough, but I'll give it my best shot. Please don't judge me if—"

His lips met mine, and I closed my eyes and felt as if I were floating because the kiss was a million times better than I'd ever hoped.

Good thing I was sitting down.

When he pulled away, I held his gaze.

"Sorry for waiting so long." He brushed his thumb over my cheek. "It has nothing to do with how I feel about you. I just don't like to be casual with my kisses."

"I appreciate that," I whispered. For once, Georgia the Babbler had nothing else to say.

He motioned to the music. "Let's hear it."

I shook myself out of the kiss-induced stupor. "I'll even sing for you." I launched into the song, and by the time I was belting out the chorus, I knew exactly what to get Cal for Christmas.

CHAPTER TWENTY-SIX

CHRISTMAS DAY

Mom and Dan loved their tandem bike. In fact, after we presented it, they bundled up and took it for a short spin around the neighborhood. It was pretty cute, watching them pedal away into the sunset.

While Mom and Dan were gone, Austin, Preston, Makayla, Dakota, Stella, and I were hanging out in the basement and drinking spiced cider while "Silver Bells" played in the background. A large pile of gifts stood next to Mom's tree that was decked with our blended family's sentimental ornaments, including many that us kids had made when we were little.

"What time is your boyfriend going to get here?" Makayla smirked.

I bit back the urge to inform her that, in spite of progressing to kissing me, he *still* hadn't made his boyfriend status official. Instead, I glanced at my watch. "Any time."

"By the way, I'm totally bummed that my idiot brothers got to be your sidekicks." She crossed her arms. "I want my turn."

I laughed and picked up some discarded wrapping paper at my feet. "I'm not making any promises, but you never know, since crimes seem to find me." Not to mention there was still Daddy's case to solve. I wadded the paper in a ball and chucked it toward the trash bag Dan had brought in.

My phone vibrated in unison with Dakota's Mario Brothers ring tone. We exchanged glances. I squealed when I saw Grandpa had sent a picture of a wrinkly hand sporting a beautiful square-cut diamond engagement ring with a simple message.

She said yes.

I showed the picture to Makayla while Dakota shared with Stella. Preston and Austin hovered over me, trying to catch a glimpse.

"I wonder if they'll have a big wedding," Makayla said.

"I doubt it." After the conversation I'd had with Grandpa in Velda's Café, I was sure he'd veto that idea.

Austin slapped my shoulder. "Whatever they do, make sure you're standing within firing distance when she tosses the bouquet. You need all the help you can get."

I rolled my eyes, and when the doorbell rang, I shot off the couch. "I'll get it." I pounded up the stairs and yanked open the door.

"Merry Christmas." Cal grinned as he stepped inside, gave me a quick peck on the lips, and slid off his coat.

"Merry Christmas." Grasping his hand, I led him into the living room where Mom's fancy tree glowed next to the fireplace. This one was full of woodland-themed ornaments. "I have a little something for you." I picked up the tiny box I'd stashed behind the tree, so the Twin Menaces wouldn't notice.

They'd taken to calling *themselves* that—as their superhero name.

Cal's eyes lit up as he ripped open the gold and white-striped package. He withdrew a strip of paper, and I held my breath while he read what I'd written.

Your gift has two parts. The first is in my truck bed.

"I thought you said it was a little something."

"Let's go."

He whistled "Jingle Bells" as we put on our coats and we went outside to the driveway. Up and down the street, houses sparkled with Christmas lights. A few stray snowflakes swirled around us in the dark, and I opened the tailgate, revealing the tarp-covered mound. "Go for it."

He lifted the cover. "A bookshelf. Look at the craftsmanship on this." He ran his hand along the edge. "It's awesome!" He hugged me so hard that he lifted my feet off the ground. "I needed a new one." Cal put me down and kissed me so enthusiastically that I was certain we were giving the neighbors a show.

Not that I cared.

A throat cleared—loudly.

Cal and I jumped away from each other.

"I take it he likes the shelf." Dan wheeled the bike up the driveway, and Mom walked beside him, grinning.

I smoothed my hair and shuffled my feet. *Merciful heavens.*

"It's perfect for my guest room." Cal's eyes sparkled.

Who knew a bookshelf could make someone so happy? I'd found an antique shelf at an estate sale—and had refinished it myself.

"I'm glad." Mom entered the code for the garage door, and she and Dan ducked inside as soon as the door had raised.

As the garage door closed, I pointed to the envelope that I'd taped to the side. "Don't forget part two."

He ripped it open and read aloud. "I'll help you unpack and organize your books." He kissed the top of my head. "That's even better since I haven't had time. Thank you."

I stood on my tiptoes and kissed his lips. "You're very welcome."

I'd taken Beverly's advice and realized Cal appreciated my help more than any gift I could ever give.

"Let's go inside so you can open *your* present," he said.

We covered the bookshelf and shut the tailgate before hurrying into the house. The shouts coming from the basement indicated Dan had insisted on playing charades. I'd never been so thankful for my stepdad's love of family games.

Cal and I settled in the living room in front of the fireplace, and he withdrew an envelope from his back pocket. "Sorry, I'm not good at wrapping."

"No worries." I tore it open and discovered two tickets for a Chanticleer concert. I squealed. "This is perfect. My favorite group, and I get to spend time with you."

"I know." His blue eyes twinkled. "That makes it a present for me too."

I laughed. The Georgia of a few months ago would've needed a barf bucket after hearing a guy make a sappy comment like that to a girl, but I didn't mind—at all—when it was directed at me.

"There's something else I've been wanting to talk to you about." He rested his hand on my face.

"Really?" My voice sounded way too squeaky to pass for cool.

He brushed a strand of hair out of my face with his thumb. "I've never asked you to be my girlfriend, but Brandi very tactfully brought it to my attention that a certain angel asked you out. And I realized I'd better make our relationship status official—that is—if you're cool with it?"

"Definitely." My breath caught as I met his intense gaze.

His lips met mine, and I moved closer.

Merry Christmas to me.

If you want to be the first to know about Georgia's next adventure, sign up for my email newsletter at www.marissashrock.com. I won't share your email with anyone. As a thank you for joining, you'll gain access to *Deadly Homestead: A Georgia Rae Winston Mini-Mystery and Other Short Stories*.

If you enjoyed *Deadly Holiday*, I'd be very grateful if you'd leave a short review to help me spread the word about my novels.

ABOUT THE AUTHOR

Jenni Mansell Photography

Marissa Shrock is a survivor of many awkward blind dates and many years of teaching middle school. Both provide excellent inspiration for her fictional yarns.

Since childhood, she's loved to read a variety of genres, so her own work includes dystopian thrillers and cozy mysteries. She's the author of the Emancipation Warriors Series and the Georgia Rae Winston Mystery Series. Her debut novel, *The First Principle*, was a Carol Award Finalist.

Marissa enjoys playing golf, building elaborate LEGO creations, and traveling to new places. Her home is in Indiana, where she's surrounded by corn and soybean fields. Visit her at www.marissashrock.com.

ALSO BY MARISSA SHROCK

Emancipation Warriors Series

The First Principle

The Liberation

The Pursuit

The Agitator: A Novella

Georgia Rae Winston Mystery Series

Deadly Harvest

Deadly Holiday

Deadly Heritage

Deadly Harmony

Deadly Hideaway

CREDITS

Editing by A Little Red Ink

Marketing Copy by JR2 Marketing & Advertising

Cover Art by Seedlings Design Studio

Cimelia Press Logo by Race Point

www.ingramcontent.com/pod-product-compliance
Lightning Source LLC
Chambersburg PA
CBHW061139170626
46809CB00003B/913